WILDLORD

PHILIP WOMACK

Little Island
Books create waves

WILDLORD

First published in 2021 by
Little Island Books
7 Kenilworth Park
Dublin 6W
Ireland

A British Library Cataloguing in Publication record for this book
is available from the British Library.

Cover by Karen Vaughan
Typeset by Kieran Nolan
Proofread by Emma Dunne
Printed in Poland by L&C

Print ISBN: 978-1-912417-97-1

Little Island has received funding to support
this book from the Arts Council of Ireland

the arts council
chomhairle ealaíon
funding literature
artscouncil.ie

10 9 8 7 6 5 4 3 2 1

For my daughters
Xenia and Amalia Womack von Preussen

Chapter 1

14th April, 1846

Look long into the eyes of a Samdhya, he said, and you shall change. I looked long. I looked deep. Blossom fell from the tree, yet I did not notice. Already, I sense myself changing.

—From the diary of Margaret Ravenswood,
daughter of the Reverend Laurence
Ravenswood, Rector of Haughley

White Quad bell rang out into the mid-morning air, and Tom Swinton slumped down onto a wooden bench underneath a statue of his school's founder. In front of him, a lone figure moved across the well-tended lawn, picking up and bagging detritus from last night's Summer Ball. Tom was still wearing his dinner jacket, his bow-tie poking out of his pocket, his top shirt buttons undone.

He closed his eyes.

The party had continued into the early hours, and he'd fallen asleep on someone's study floor, wrapped in a duvet. Sunlight had woken him at dawn. His friends were snoring gently, sprawled on their beds or on rugs. He'd gone to walk in the woods, which he always liked to do, taking with him a cold can from a vending machine.

He wanted to be alone among the trees. He hadn't wanted to say goodbye to anyone. He'd wandered around the grounds for hours, making the fizzy drink last, waiting until he was sure all the cars, with their loads of schoolbooks and sports clothes and teenage boys, had gone.

Now, sinking back, the hard slats of the bench pressing into him, he counted the tolls of the bells.

8, 9, 10 …

It was almost eleven o'clock, and at some point he would have to properly face the fact that he was the only pupil left in the whole school, for the entire summer holidays.

A cough made him look up. A boy he didn't recognise was standing on the gravel path in front of him. Almost eight hundred boys attended the school. Tom, being in the lower sixth form, did not come across many of the younger ones; but he knew most of them by sight. There was something distinctive about this one, though, and Tom wondered why he hadn't noticed him around. He would have remembered him.

Tom couldn't tell how old the boy was. He was very pale, with short black hair oddly combed so that it lay almost flat to his skull, and a snub nose. He looked like he might be in one of the junior forms, but a challenge in his eyes suggested otherwise.

Big fawn's eyes and long trembling lashes. His uniform didn't quite fit him, the purple jacket with its absurd gold stripes hanging off his shoulders; his tie in the school colours, green and grey, done up askew.

The badge on his blazer was odd. Instead of the school crest it showed a small square inside another square and another one inside that.

The boy was holding something to his chest, arms tightly across it. Tom wasn't in the mood to be disturbed and savagely dragged a hand through his long blond hair, letting it fall across his eyes before blowing it away in displeasure. 'Shouldn't you have left?' he snapped. 'Everyone else has.'

The boy didn't reply. Instead, he uncrossed his arms and offered up what was in his hands.

At first Tom ignored him. But there was a tightness in the boy's shoulders. An insistence.

Tom took it carefully.

It was a letter. A heavy cream envelope of a type Tom hadn't seen for years. The address was written in spidery ink.

'Where did you get this?' Tom straightened. 'Did you take it from my pidge?' The boy didn't answer.

It was clearly addressed to him:

> Master Thos. Swinton
> Downshire College

There was no postcode, no county.

The boy shifted slightly, as if expecting something. Tom continued to stare at the letter. There was a silence around him; everything seemed so still, and he could hear no birds.

3

Even the litter-picker seemed to have paused, deep in thought, and a cloud hung partway over the sun.

Thos? What did that mean? Nobody had ever called him *Thos*.

He turned the heavy letter over and was surprised to see that it was sealed with scarlet wax, which bore the imprint of a heraldic animal like a leopard's head. He didn't want to break the seal, but after a second's thought, he slid his finger under it and opened the letter, leaving the body of the wax intact.

There was a single piece of thick card inside and two other small bits of orange card which fluttered out. Tom caught them without giving them a glance.

The writing was hard to decipher, flowery and scratchy, with flourishes in unexpected places. Somebody had spent a long time writing this letter. The boy, standing patiently in front of him, scratched his nose. Tom struggled to make out the writing.

Mundham Farm
Mundham
Suffolk

To my well-beloved cousin Thomas James Swinton,

You will come to stay with me, your dear Uncle James who has thought of you for so long and with such hope.

There is not much here but it is time for you to see and time for you to understand.

4

There are many things that I need you to do and many things that you shall need to learn.

You are the only other Swinton who remains.

Zita has arranged everything. You shall use the coupons herein. I am to hope that you shall know and do what is required. You shall be met at the post.

I remain, your most affectionate uncle,

James Swinton, Esquire

It was signed with an elaborate, curlicued swoop.

Uncle? Tom didn't have an uncle. At least, nobody had ever told him he had an uncle. His father had been an only child. Could this James Swinton be a great-uncle? No, his grandfather only had sisters, and they'd changed their names when they'd got married, and as far as he knew those cousins were ranching in Australia or playing golf in Canada.

He looked more closely at the cards he held in his hand. A train ticket – a single one – and a receipt for it. Paid in cash, he noted. On the back of the receipt were scribbled the names of his stops, in different, more conventional handwriting.

It was for tomorrow. The 09.03 from Houghton to London, a quick change on the underground to Liverpool Street Station, where he had to get off, then a train on to Colchester, and then another change to a small station he assumed was in Suffolk. Mundham must be near enough to it.

5

What did 'You will be met at the post' mean? Maybe there was a post office outside the station where you waited. It could be local slang. He didn't know anything about Suffolk. The whole thing was very strange.

Tom sensed a shadow passing over him.

He looked up. He had forgotten about the boy who'd delivered the letter.

But there was no boy. There had been no crunch of gravel on the path as he'd left.

The quad bell was still ringing: ... ii.

The litter-picker finished his stretching and began to cross the lawn once more. Clouds scudded across the sky.

All this had happened in the gap between the bell sounding the tenth and the eleventh stroke.

Chapter 2

16th April, 1846

Today, he told me his name. As far as I can transliterate it here, it is Rohenga, which means in his tongue Hawk in the Mist. When he says it, my heart dances.

—From the diary of Margaret Ravenswood

The school's emptiness flowed around Tom like an echo, pouring down the colonnaded sides of White Quad and washing over the stone cloisters. In the shade of the single plane tree, he gripped the letter tightly and then, fearful of crumpling it, smoothed it out flat on his knees. His dinner jacket felt hot on him, and he shifted it off, letting it fall in a rumpled mess to his side.

Where usually there would be the shouts and stampedes of boys on their way to lessons or games or meals, now there was nothing. Only the college mowers were humming distantly. A master, white head down and gnarled hands held tightly behind his back, black gown flapping, hurrying to some not-wished-for appointment, caught sight of Tom. He paused, knuckled his hands on his hips and shouted,

'Go and get changed, Swinton, you're a disgrace,' before scurrying onwards in the direction of the headmaster's house. Tom stood. He would go back to his room.

A couple of house matrons were chatting by the door to Tom's boarding house. One of them, with a rabbity face and a faint antiseptic scent of the sanatorium, eyed him askance and looked like she was about to say something. Tom made a mock bow, grabbed her by the shoulders and kissed her lightly on the cheek, skipped down the stairs and passed through the heavy oak door.

Eight weeks of holidays stretched ahead of Tom. Eight weeks in which he was bound to stay here in school. His nearest friend lived a twenty-mile drive away, beyond the Downs; but Tom couldn't drive and didn't have a car. Anyway, Fred was doing internships at the local newspaper office and with the borough's MP. Fred had his sights set on Oxbridge – he always had done. 'And when I'm not working, I'll be revising,' he'd said the day before, potting a ball as they'd played a final game of pool. 'We need these holidays to consolidate for our exams. Beat you again.'

Tom wished he had his own sights set on something. Instead, when he looked into his future after school, he just saw a blank space.

He stomped through the empty boarding house to his tiny study and slumped onto the hard bed.

An hour or so later, a pasty, spotty face poked round the door, staring through thick-rimmed glasses and topped with a mass of oily, unruly brown curls.

Tom, showered and changed into blue jeans and an old white T-shirt, was sitting on his wooden chair by the window. His room looked out onto School Quad, and Tom was alternately gazing out at the bricks and studying the letter. He placed it as unhurriedly as he could into his pocket and kicked his shabby canvas trainers against each other, nonchalantly.

'Swinton, Fletch wants you,' said the face, scratched its nose, scowled and vanished, banging the door shut as Tom shouted, 'You could have knocked!' after him.

Tom caught up with the third-former scurrying along the lower-sixth-form corridor, which still stank of spray deodorants and mustiness. All the doors to the narrow, Spartan study bedrooms were open; and all of them were empty, the posters recently torn down, leaving tiny imprints behind them where they'd been stuck up with Blu Tack or tape.

'Why does he want me?'

'Didn't say,' said the boy, who was Colin Fletcher, the youngest son of Tom's housemaster. They came clattering down the wooden stairs and reached the House Hall.

A tall mullioned window lent brightness to the rows of boards showing house honours, names painted onto wood, and the rack of pigeon holes, all now empty.

The boy hung for a moment on the banisters and gaped at Tom, until Tom shooed him away.

He checked his pidge, as if there might be something there to explain the letter; but all that was in it was a pink form he had yet to fill in about his university choices for next year. He put it back without looking at it.

A second later he knocked on Fletcher's door and heard the housemaster's deep response: 'Enter!' There was rather too much emphasis on the first syllable. Fletch sometimes liked to showboat, and Tom was one of the few who didn't humour him. He went in sulkily.

The housemaster was ensconced in his large, comfortable brown leather armchair, which took up most of the office. He was a bulky man, with sparse grey hair and red-veined cheeks. Shining rugby trophies cluttered the shelves, which were largely bare of books. A plant pot occupied most of the remaining space. The very small window was wide open.

Fletcher was in his shirtsleeves. A fan on his desk was purring, but sweat patches were showing under his arms, darkening his blue shirt. Every time the fan moved across him, his tie, hanging loosely from an open collar, flapped.

'Could do better,' said Fletch to himself, in his peculiarly nasal voice, hardly looking up from the reports he was writing with a thick fountain pen. 'Sometimes I wish I could write what I really think. But I don't think parents want to hear that, do they, Swinton?' Fletcher placed his pen on top of a pile of papers as if it were a weapon. He folded his arms deliberately. 'There have been rumours this term – which I am willing to believe are only rumours. You have one year left here at Downshire and you are all set to do well in your A Levels. There are universities to apply to, internships to get. I am willing to give you the BOD.' He liked to use sporting references.

Tom said nothing; he crossed his legs at the ankle.

'But –' and here Fletcher pointed his large nose at Tom, beetling his brows together '– if, whilst you are here under my guardianship over this holiday, I find any evidence of anything – *anything* – that might point to the truth of these rumours, I need leave you in no doubt that school rules will apply.' He paused significantly. If his eyebrows could get any closer together, Tom thought, they might join up and become one. 'You will be considered for expulsion.' He let the word hang in the air. His tie flapped, as if in emphasis. 'For the moment, though, you will be gated and can only leave the school grounds with *adult*' – a word he unnecessarily stressed – 'supervision. Last chance, Swinton. Last chance.'

Tom thought about the half bottle of whiskey that he and a friend had snuck in half a term ago one Saturday afternoon. Fletch must have smelled it on them at roll call before dinner. He gave his best 'I don't know what you're talking about' grin.

'Sir – it's the holidays. Aren't I even allowed to go into town on my own for a kebab?'

Fletch furrowed his brow even further. 'No, Swinton, you are not allowed to go into town for a … kebab. Go on healthy walks. Admire the rolling countryside. Perhaps even you, Tom Swinton, could find it in yourself to use the extensive sports facilities. And always, always, always sign in with me, after breakfast, at lunch, at 6.30pm and at 10.30pm. Do you understand me?'

A giggle sounded behind him, and Tom knew that the Fletcher boy was hanging about outside, listening in.

Prison wasn't too strong a word. 'That's …'

'That's that, Master Swinton. I can't have you causing me trouble during the holidays as well as during term time. Now I've got to write these bloody reports. I've done yours already, before you ask.' With a gesture, he left Tom in no doubt as to the content, turning it into a dismissive motion, and Tom departed with as much dignity as he could hope to muster.

The Fletcher boy was hanging about in the corridor. Tom resisted the urge to glare at him.

He remembered the letter in his pocket and turned round to knock on the door again. Could he show it to Fletcher? It was a way out, after all.

One look at the third-former picking his nose firmed his resolve.

Chapter 3

16th April, 1846

They have many names for themselves. Sometimes they are the Storm, sometimes the Deep. When the Wildlord rides, they are the Wildmark.

— From the diary of Margaret Ravenswood

Back in the housemaster's office, Fletcher took and read Tom's letter carefully. 'This looks like you concocted it in the art room.'

'It was in my pidge, sir,' said Tom, knowing he couldn't tell the truth about the strange boy with his tie askew and the way that time had seemed to stop.

Had stopped.

No, it couldn't have done. The bell tolled again in his mind, and the boy's dark eyes flashed at him.

'We–ell… there's no postmark or stamp. And there's no phone number on this letter, Swinton. Let alone an email address. I can't contact this man who says he's your uncle. I can't let you go.' He steepled his hands together, cracking his large beefy knuckles. 'Much as I would like to have you off my conscience.'

'But the train – it's tomorrow morning.'

'I will have to write to him myself and receive a confirmation from both him and from your guardian. You say yourself that you haven't heard of this James Swinton.'

Tom shook his head. 'I … I remember something. James Swinton, my uncle. I remember dad talking about it …' He trailed off. The truth was he didn't. There had been some vague talk in the family about a Suffolk farm. What had it been called? Mundham? It sounded fairly familiar. As he watched Fletch frowning, he dimly caught at the back of his mind the sound of his mother mentioning it.

His father had never talked about it, though, or any of his relations. And now he'd never have the chance to ask him, as both his parents had been dead, drowned, at the bottom of the Atlantic Ocean, for the last five years.

'Your guardian's in Hong Kong, isn't he?' Fletch turned to his computer and began tapping with one finger, searching for his contact details. 'I'll bung him an email and we'll see what he has to say.'

'Sir – he won't answer in time. He's too busy. And I don't have any money. If I'm going to go, I need to go on this ticket.'

'Ah.' Fletcher fiddled with his tie. 'Found the fellow.'

'Look – why would he send me a ticket if he wasn't legitimate?'

A rare look of sympathy passed over Fletch's face. He puffed out his enormous cheeks and waggled his giant eyebrows.

'Master Swinton,' he sighed. 'I'm tied up here with reports. I've got to get them out by the end of the day, or there'll be the worst kind of stinking hell to pay from the Head Man.'

'Sir – please ...'

Fletcher seemed to relent a little. 'Steady, Swinton, hold your horses. I'll phone your guardian later and do some looking into this Jack Swinton. And if he turns out all right, I'll lend you the money for the train. Which will be taken out of your house account, of course. All right?' He sighed, turned back to his pile of reports and uncapped his pen, holding the nib above the page for a second. Then, firmly, he recapped it.

Tenderness did not come easily to Fletcher. He cleared his throat. 'I know you've had a difficult time. And I know that part of your ... challenging behaviour has been because of ... because of what happened to your parents. And we have made allowances for that.'

Tom burned inside.

'But I can't have you causing trouble. All right?' The matter was gone, dealt with. He turned back to his reports.

It wasn't all right. None of it was. Tom felt like smashing the pen from Fletch's hand.

But he didn't.

Later, after a desultory supper of sausages and mashed potato, cooked by Fletch's surprisingly kindly wife, where the three young Fletchers had largely ignored him, Tom gratefully slipped away to his house TV room, preferring not to be in his study.

He sat watching old comedies, about people living complicated lives in New York apartments, so far removed from his own. He slowly picked through a packet of crisps and sipped at a can of Coke, till he had to sign in at 10.30pm.

Fletch barely glanced at him when he turned up at 10.32pm. He was still finishing his reports.

Tom skulked on up to his bedroom. The stairs creaked loudly as he went. His whole corridor was dark and empty. Sitting down on his narrow bed, ready to get undressed, he felt exposed, as if he were the only person in the whole school.

He thought of the almost silent dinner, the few questions from Mrs Fletcher, which he'd answered in short sentences. The repeats on TV. There were only so many series he could watch on his laptop without getting bored.

He couldn't stay here and do this every night.

The moon was out, casting School Quad with a gentle glow, whilst the lamps that lit the quad's sides were being turned off one by one. His was the only light in the upper floors.

If Fletch wouldn't let him go tomorrow, there was only one thing he could do. He would have to sneak out.

He looked again at the tickets that had come with the letter. It was clear to him. He had to get that train.

The station was about three miles' walk away. It took a bit less than an hour if you went through the back lanes. But he would attract suspicion if he was seen walking down there in the morning with a bag.

So he would have to hide one in a bush by the gate tonight and pick it up on his way tomorrow.

There was a back route out of the school, a path that went down through the farmer's fields, and there was a stile leading on to the road that went to the village.

By the time they noticed he'd gone it would be too late to catch him, and he'd be on his way to Mundham Farm.

He would do it. Filled with sudden energy, he found a small rucksack and packed it with a week's worth of clothes and a toothbrush and his mobile phone charger and a couple of books. He also placed in it a small folder, in which he kept a photograph of himself with his mother and father, and a few other keepsakes, including notes and cards they had written to him.

He tried not to look at the photograph for too long.

Tom waited, reading and scrolling through messages on his phone, until White Quad bell had struck midnight, and then crept down the corridor to the stairs to the tower door, which led outside.

He would go down to the stile now, hide the bag and be back without anyone noticing.

The night was still and the short stretch of grass between him and the path was cast into silver. To his right, Fletcher's rooms were mostly darkened. A light shone in what must have been one of the older boys' rooms, and he could hear the faint bleeps and calls of a multi-player computer game in progress. There was a tremendous coughing, and Tom saw the silhouette of his housemaster behind the screen of his bathroom blind.

As soon as Tom got onto the path that led to the farmer's fields, he had a sudden sensation that the school had entirely vanished and that he was alone, surrounded by nothing but darkness for miles.

To reassure himself, he turned and saw the bulk of the school building looming as it always had done, angular and vast.

As the school receded into the darkness while he walked onwards, he started to feel almost lighthearted. Any worries he might have had about being discovered, or what might happen when Fletcher found out he had absconded, disappeared into the cool night. He whistled and was delighted to hear an owl hooting in what seemed like response.

He came to a place where the scrubby path curved and passed round the bend, stretching a hand out to lop off the top of a tall grass and letting the feathery part idly fall to the ground.

In the middle of the path, draped in a long cloak, someone was standing, facing away from him. Tom halted.

Could it be one of the masters, out for a night stroll? Hardly likely. It might be the farmer. Or it might be a would-be burglar casing the school.

But that cloak. No farmer or burglar would wear a cloak.

The figure was tall, and unusually slender. Tom would have to pass by it to carry on; either that or he'd have to scramble through the hedge on his right and make his way through the field.

Cloak swirling, the figure turned.

In the moonlight, Tom could make out every individual feature on his face. The man's hair was carefully held back in a ponytail. Though he was smiling, it was not with warmth. He had a tattoo on his cheek, in startling scarlet, of a long-tailed, tufty-eared creature that might have been a leopard. As the man stepped nearer to Tom, and bowed, in a courtly, slightly mocking way, the tattoo seemed to dance.

'We have known you were here,' he said. His accent was hard to place.

The man stretched forwards as if to grasp him by the throat, but stopped, his fingers a few inches away from Tom's skin.

'Stay here, Thomas James Swinton. Stay here, and do not wake the past.' He bowed again, and then stood up straight, ears pricked, as if he could sense something on the wind. His nostrils curved, and the leopard tattoo – or was it Tom's imagination? – stretched and flexed its forelegs. When he bared his lips now, his teeth were sharp, and Tom had the powerful sense that he was in the presence of a wild beast.

'Who are you? How did you know I was here? How… how did you know my name?' He stumbled over the words. He felt at once as if he wanted to flee and that he wanted to stay with this person for ever.

'Too many questions.'

It happened quickly. There was a flash of bronze metal; the man snarled and slashed at Tom, leaving a long, bright red mark on his forearm. Terrified, Tom sprang backwards, the pain sudden and sharp, the blood welling through his fingers as he clutched at the wound. A breeze from the sea rustled the crops, and a drop of blood fell and stained his trainers.

Growling, his attacker sprang away into the darkness.

19

Chapter 4

18th April, 1846

Today, Rohenga held a leaf up to the light, and showed me the tracings within it. 'That is what we are. The Samdhya. The Holding Together.' He laughed and threw the leaf away onto the wind. I wanted to keep it, as he had once touched it, but I could not watch where it fell.

—From the diary of Margaret Ravenswood

Tom hefted his bag on his shoulder as he stood on the platform at Holt. The wound on his forearm had shaken him, although it was only skin deep; it had caused a fair amount of blood, and he had thrown his T-shirt away, before bandaging up the cut and spraying it with disinfectant he'd found in the matron's office.

Perversely, the encounter had made him all the keener to go to his uncle's farm, and so, after the strange figure had gone, he had left his bag in the hedge anyway, and the next morning, without telling Fletch, had picked it up and made it to the station by 9.03, just as the train pulled in to the platform, half-empty apart from a few people on their way to go shopping or see the sights in London. It was a Saturday.

He'd found a quiet place in a corner and settled in with his music. The air was clear, and the sun shone through the glass onto his face. A family of four played cards at the table seats near him, laughing and joking. He watched Downshire, still visible on its hill, until it dwindled away.

The weather had got progressively worse as the train neared London, grey clouds gathering.

Tom was not used to the Underground and went in the wrong direction on the Central Line for two stops; but he eventually arrived at Liverpool Street Station, where he bought a bacon sandwich and a too hot coffee. The clamour of people hurrying by made him feel insignificant. Men and women in suits stomped past, phones clamped to their ears or peering into tiny screens.

He'd caught the train heading east with two minutes to spare, and the sky was bruising yellow.

Holt Station was small; nobody else alighted from the tiny branch-line train he'd taken from Colchester, and as it rattled away, he realised he did not know who was going to pick him up, only that he would be met at the post. Would it be James himself, he wondered, and pictured some kindly old buffer in fraying tweeds and wellies, a fat black labrador at his feet.

There was a guard in the station office, behind a plastic grille, counting off something on a clipboard. Tom asked him if he knew Mundham Farm, but the guard only shrugged and looked at him suspiciously.

Even now his phone was vibrating with messages. Fletch had clocked he'd gone at signing-in time.

Tom had put off listening to them till now. He paused outside the empty waiting room, then braced himself and accessed the voicemails.

Fletcher, of course, calling him every name under the sun, begging him to call as soon as possible. Three messages. He deleted them all.

And a surprise. His guardian, Hector Tsang, calling from across the world.

Tom bit his lip.

He could hardly make out what Hector was saying for a moment, the line was so crackly. Disappointment that Tom had left without asking him for permission. Annoyance at the trouble he was causing.

Then a pause, and a gap, in which Hector was clearly addressing someone else about some deal or other. Another crackle, and Tom heard '...James Swinton, yesterday. As far as I'm concerned, Tom, you can stay there at Mundham, and if you need anything, don't forget to ask my secretary – you've got her email, I think. She'll...' The message broke off, and was followed by another, slightly disappointed one from Fletcher, asking Tom to send him confirmation of the address.

With a flash of triumph, Tom texted it to Fletch, then, after a second of remorse, followed it with an apology. He shoved his phone back into his jeans pocket. His uncle must have squared his guardian earlier. He wondered if a similar letter had arrived and what the businesslike Hector would have made of it. He'd probably just shifted it over to his secretary and let her deal with it. Tom thought of the white, airless office, the trolleys stuffed with expensive food, the hum of quiet voices, the fluorescent lights.

Eleven o'clock, his uncle had said. And now it was 10.52. He kicked his feet together. He was bleary from not sleeping properly, and his stomach was annoyingly empty. The cut on his arm itched just a little, and he tried not to scratch it. He could do with a bacon sandwich and some hot, sweet tea.

There was a café on the platform. He went up to the door hopefully; though the sign said OPEN, it was locked, and a white-shirted employee scrubbing tables inside only glanced up at him when he knocked on the door, making no move to open it. Her eyes heavy, she simply looked back down and continued her work.

Tom was searching for a vending machine, jingling the coins in his pocket, when an unfamiliar noise made him look towards the road.

The slow tread of shod hooves on tarmac. Coming up the narrow road into the station was a large black horse, its nostrils flaring, and attached to the horse, by a leather harness, was a cart.

Sitting perched uncomfortably and as upright as a tree trunk on the driver's seat, dressed, or rather swathed, in thick black clothes, was what appeared to be a finely featured young woman; but as the cart drew nearer, and the horse and cart came to a slow halt in front of Tom, he saw that it was in fact a boy of about his own age.

The boy moved slowly, almost as slowly as the horse, and when he turned and looked fully at Tom, Tom could hardly help drawing in his breath sharply.

His eyes were silver. The irises were not grey, as Tom had seen before in one or two boys at school, but a dull silver.

And so, underneath his black wide-brimmed hat, was his hair, a metallic gleam unlike anything Tom had ever known.

The horse blew out its nostrils. The boy made no sign of encouragement, apart from to point at Tom and then at the seat beside him.

Looking about for a car, Tom said, 'I'm waiting for my uncle to pick me up?'

The boy simply repeated the gesture, in his slow way.

Tom bridled a little, wondering if he was mocking him. 'I... I don't mean to be rude, but...'

Raindrops pattered his cheeks. There was a train back to London in an hour or so. He couldn't see a pub or even a house, apart from a small dilapidated cottage, on which a sign said, optimistically: *Ben's Taxis. Airport Service.*

From the back of the cart, a little head poked out. It was a dog; a lurcher, black-headed and white-throated, with soft, bright eyes. The rain was getting harder.

'You're from James Swinton, my uncle? I'm Tom, Tom Swinton. Thomas. Er, Thos.' He wasn't sure if you said that with a *th* or a *t*. Awkwardly, Tom stuck out his hand, but the boy ignored it, instead nodding slightly and gesturing again.

What choice did Tom really have? The worst that could happen would be that if he arrived at the farm and hated it, he could phone a taxi, if Ben wasn't off delivering people to airports. So he glanced back at the platform. The ticket seller had come out and was standing stolidly, arms folded, with a vacant look on his face. The woman in the café was still scrubbing; she did not stop to watch. Perhaps she was used to horses and carts picking people up at the station.

Deciding, Tom swung himself up onto the seat, settling his bag under his feet, and turned to tickle the dog's tummy. She stretched herself out delightedly, closing her eyes in pleasure. She had a little white star on the top of her head, and he scratched it, letting her lick his face.

The boy had remained entirely still for the whole time. He took the reins, and the horse, who clearly knew its driver well, turned heavily and clopped slowly out to the road.

They didn't stay on it for very long, turning onto a broad bridleway a short way from the station. The sun was entirely hidden by clouds, but the leaves of the trees rustled and woodpigeons cooed. The rain tailed off.

The journey, to begin with, was silent. But as they moved further away from the station, the boy began to soften a little. After they'd trundled off into a single-track road, a holloway almost tunnel-like with green, he lifted his silver eyes to Tom and said, 'Kit. I be named Kit.'

He had a low, strong Suffolk burr. The dog whimpered.

'She doesn't want to be forgotten,' said Tom. 'What's her name?'

There was a long pause before Kit replied. The cartwheels rolled and the horse's hooves hit the ruts steadily; the beast snorted once, swatting his tail from side to side. 'Leana,' said Kit, and then, as if the effort had been too great for him, he turned away and kept his silver eyes on the track.

After what felt to Tom to be at least an hour, but was probably more like half, horse and cart turned into an even narrower road, bordered on both sides by thick hedgerows. Tom could hear the faintest sound of music on the breeze. A pipe, it seemed. The sound of it made Kit stiffen, and he urged his horse onwards. The horse began to trot.

The house now came into view. Tom would have liked to stop to take it in. But the cart was now trundling faster.

It was a farmhouse; not really as Tom had expected it. It was built from red brick, tumbledown and sprawling, looming from its position on a small island surrounded by a narrow moat. There were two storeys and what looked like a small attic above. Tall mullioned windows. Around it spread fields, mostly grassed over and ill kept. Through the branches of a copse, the crest of a small mound poked upwards.

Something moved on top of it; there was a whooshing sound, and Tom, astonished, looked down at his hand.

Right next to it, buried into the wood, fletched with a black feather, was an arrow.

Kit moved the horse on faster and now they were properly trotting; now cantering and another arrow whizzed and thudded into the wooden slats of the cart. Tom ducked down, clutching his arms over his head; and then, as he trembled, unable to see anything, he felt the horse slowing to a walk once more.

Tom heard a crunch as Kit jumped down onto gravel. They must have arrived in front of the farmhouse. The danger – whatever it was – must have passed. Gingerly, he peered over the side of the cart and saw Kit carefully shutting a gate at the end of a short bridge. They'd crossed the moat and were on the island.

'What the ...' Tom sat back. 'What was that?' Leana licked his hand. Kit merely beckoned with a long finger.

Tom, shaking with adrenaline, lowered himself onto the badly gravelled drive, swung his rucksack down and was immensely grateful for Leana, who flowed down next to him and hovered, as if protectively, by his legs.

The mound could be seen to the east; but there was no shadow on it now. Tom pulled the arrow out of the wood. It was beautifully made. Kit gently took it from him and stalked up to the front door.

Tom jogged to follow him, and soon he was stepping past a battered heavy wooden door, into the gloom of a stone hall.

It was quite large. There were paintings on the walls and a fireplace with a fire blazing, despite the season, brocaded chairs on either side. There was a smell of damp. He suddenly felt the cold and rubbed his arms. The silver-haired boy had vanished. Four lit candles stood on a windowsill. He stood uncertainly, his bag clutched in his hand.

A voice came from the shadows.

'Thomas Swinton. Welcome, Thomas Swinton. Welcome home at last.'

The hall filled with his name.

27

Two people were standing on the further side.

'Isn't Kit a darling?' drawled another voice, and one of them came forwards. 'How splendid!' It was a girl, with short dark hair tied with a white bow, wearing a black dress that didn't look like it should be worn on a farm. She was thin and pale and had huge dark shadows under her eyes. 'Oh, how spiffing, what fun we shall have!' She clapped her hands and twirled. 'What a party we shall make!' She looked Tom up and down, making him feel uncomfortable. There was something familiar about her eyes. 'I do hope your journey wasn't too unbearable.'

Tom felt his tongue seem to grow thick. 'Just now – an arrow, shooting at us? Shooting at – me?' Nobody shot arrows any more – did they? Maybe it was some re-enactment thing. He'd seen pictures in the papers of men and women dressing up in the uniforms of armies gone by. Civil War stuff, maybe, or even further back. This was exactly the kind of place where they would do such things, he thought. It might even have been some costume drama, using the house as a backdrop. But there hadn't been any vans or cameras.

The other person stepped forwards, and for a moment Tom's heart rose. Something in the lineaments of the man's face reminded him of his father: the way that the eyes, round and bright, were set above high cheekbones, the long, pale tapering hands, the set of the shoulders. He faltered.

It was obviously James Swinton. The girl's lip curled faintly as James put a hand on her shoulder. He wore fawn britches and long white stockings and a white shirt that sagged loosely around his thin frame, with black leather shoes whose long tongues poked upwards.

'Come nearer,' whispered James. There was a strange, haggard beauty to his face. His cheeks were hollow, his blue eyes bright with energy, his hair white and thick.

'You're a Swinton all right,' said James. The man's voice was soothing. 'Come nearer.'

Tom, a little relieved, inched forwards until he was within arm's reach.

James peered and took Tom's chin between his fingers and thumb.

After a few seconds, as if satisfied, he let go, muttering again, 'You're a Swinton all right. William Swinton's child. My ... nephew.' He said 'nephew' as if it had a V in it. The girl moved about the room, drifting like a feather. Smoke curled from the fire and something was roasting nearby. Through the window, the breeze stirred the tops of trees.

'A wondrous day. This is a wondrous day for Mundham Farm. And for the Swintons.' He smiled, as if with a great effort. 'You are home now, Thomas Swinton. Home. And there is much here for you. My dear Zita will show you everything. I must work. But I will meet you for a drink before supper tonight.' He said 'tonight' with great emphasis, then grasped Tom's hand once more.

'Thank, you, er, James.'

'Jack. Call me Jack, dear boy.' He shook Tom's hand weakly, and then shuffled off around a corner and was gone.

So much for the cheery old buffer in a waxed jacket, thought Tom. The light in the room seemed to alter slightly after Jack had left. Sunbeams now striped the stone floor. Tom turned to Zita, who was scowling, and said, 'What about that arrow? Shouldn't we be calling the police?'

'Oh, I wouldn't bother with them. It's just a little … local difficulty,' sighed Zita.

'Trespassers?' said Tom.

'If you want to think of it like that.'

That was all he got out of her. When he asked her if it was safe to go outside, she simply glared at him, fiddled with her white bow and said, 'Don't be so ridiculously stupid. Of course it is.'

At least James seemed friendly, thought Tom. Jack. His uncle. He wondered what he might know about his mother and father and resolved to ask him that night at dinner.

Zita took him upstairs, sighing theatrically as she did so. There was a long corridor and she led him along it, coming to a low wooden door, and showed him into the room that was going to be his.

She hovered on the threshold. The room was quite large and clean, with a high wood-framed single bed and a small uncomfortable-looking armchair upholstered in green. A porcelain washstand occupied one corner, with soap and a toothmug. Somebody had prepared the room for him, Tom thought. Dark oil paintings hung on the walls, of horses, hounds and rugged landscapes and one of a severe-looking woman dressed in black, which looked to be from the seventeenth century. She had a fierce expression and she was pointing downwards.

A bookshelf ran along the bottom of the window, on which were china figurines of people and birds and a few ancient books bound in red leather with the Swinton crest stamped on them in gold. The lurcher slipped in past him and leapt up onto the blankets as if she'd always been there.

'Oh, is this your bed?' Tom moved to tickle her under the chin, and she lay, luxuriously, allowing him to stroke her belly.

When he turned back to the door, Zita had gone. Tom unpacked his few belongings whilst the lurcher watched him, ears pricked up. Then, exhausted suddenly, he lay down on the bed next to her, and she curled into his side.

He was filled with a warmth he hadn't felt for a long time. Maybe this was what he'd been looking for. Maybe this really was home. The house seemed to breathe gently around him, and the swaying of the trees outside lulled him. He drifted off into sleep, warmed by a patchwork silk-edged coverlet that he pulled over himself and the dog, her breathing steady, her legs twitching as she chased after deer in her dreams.

Chapter 5

18th April, 1846

The Samdhya see everything at once. He tried to explain to me, but I could not understand him. I told him my fears for the future. He said, 'There is no future.' I lost my pearl hatpin in the woods.

—From the diary of Margaret Ravenswood

Tom's empty stomach woke him a couple of hours later. Downstairs, the grandfather clock chimed three times. The sun had come out fully now, and warm beams lay across the wooden floor and the dark red Persian rug that covered about half of it.

Leana had gone, and Tom, missing her, stumbled out onto the shadowy, dusty landing. A large spider scuttled away at his steps.

He wondered if there might be some family portraits or documents that he would be able to look into. Maybe there would be pictures of his father and grandfather. He hoped he might be able to find something; he knew so little about the Swintons.

Many wooden doors led off the corridor, and a rickety flight went up to what he assumed must be an attic. He had a curious sense that there were more doors than there had been when Zita had shown him to his room. There was plenty to explore, plenty to occupy him for the summer.

The whole house was lit with warmth. Delicious cooking smells were coming from somewhere, and he paused at the foot of the attic stairs, his stomach leading him on. He sprang down, hoping to find the kitchen.

On the other side of the entrance hall was a door that led into a bright, sunlit kitchen. It was kitted out like any farmhouse kitchen, with a large sink and a range. Pots and pans hung from hooks, and bunches of herbs. The scent was pleasant and welcoming.

Zita was sitting at the table, eating stew from a willow-patterned china bowl with a silver spoon, and Kit was with her. Zita nodded at a chipped bowlful on the table, and Tom helped himself, filling a bowl to the brim with the soft-looking meat and dark gravy.

After the first few mouthfuls, he felt a lot better. Even Kit's silver eyes and hair seemed, in the light of this warm room, almost normal. As Zita moved about, placing dishes in the sink and checking things in the larder, Tom relaxed. He smiled, but Kit wouldn't catch his eyes.

Tom turned to Zita instead.

'What can we do this afternoon?'

'He'ull be wi' me,' said Kit thickly.

Zita looked up sharply from where she was counting eggs in a bowl. 'Darling,' she said, 'dear old Jack said –'

'Jack said he'd be put to work.'

'And so he will, helping me in the woods.'

'My work's more important n'yours.'

To Tom's astonishment, Zita snarled, a proper, vicious snarl, like a stoat, and the lurcher, who had, ghost-like, slipped in beside Tom, whimpered.

'Finish.' Kit spoke through a mouthful, then pushed his bowl away.

The kitchen door burst open, and Uncle Jack came through, hobbling a little. He greeted Tom cheerfully, and Tom inquired after his afternoon's work. The old man stared at him keenly.

'Now, now, do not talk of work. We must not get to work so soon. You must rest. It is time for us to enjoy each other's presence for a while. Thomas Swinton, my dear Thomas Swinton.'

He sauntered to a decanter full of dark liquid that stood ready on a side table, and unsteadily poured out portions into four small crystal glasses. 'Although I am the master, I do like to do some things myself,' he said, smiling at Tom. 'You will find us a tightly run household, but a merry one too.'

Tom caught Zita glaring in the reflection in the window. She quickly adjusted her features and, when she turned, she too was smiling.

'Yes, we do have quite the beanfeast most days.' She took a glass from the tray and passed it to Tom.

'Thank you.' Tom sipped. It was port, delicious and velvety, and he drank it down in two gulps. 'Kit did say something about being put to work. I'd love to help – whatever you need. What kind of farming do you do here?'

Zita snorted, then recovered herself.

'More later, later, my boy. First, allow me to show you around the house.' Jack drained his glass and clasped his hands together, then stood in a way in which Tom's father, William, used to stand, upright and with his shoulders squared. Spindly and crane-like, the old man beamed. He bowed, opening the door for Tom to go through first.

As they moved, Jack became more sprightly. He delighted in telling Tom about the pictures in the main hall, and in the small, relatively cosy sitting room that led off it. There was no television there, and no radio that he could see. A wooden door set underneath the stairs went down to the cellar.

'You won't need to be going in there,' said Jack. 'Although Zita does enjoy her wine.'

There was a definite countryfied tang to his accent, thought Tom, much less pronounced than Kit's, but still there. Jack must have been living here for years, almost a recluse, without company apart from Zita and Kit.

Jack's rooms on the first floor were all the way at the end of the corridor. As they approached the door, something lively entered his gait, and he pushed it open with ease.

The space was unlike anything Tom had ever seen before. He could not help letting out a gasp of appreciation.

35

Jack seemed to enjoy this and went through, muttering quietly to himself.

Tom paused on the threshold to take it in. It occupied one whole side of the house, with large mullioned windows looking out over the scrubby, weedy lawn below, across the clear water of the moat and over the unkempt fields towards the woods beyond. There was another door, which Tom presumed led to a bedroom. A profusion of vials, some filled with dark liquids, covered the whole of one surface. Shelves lined every wall right up to the ceiling, and each shelf was bursting with volumes, some tatty and ancient, others glowing with bright bindings.

From the ceiling hung a glass box. It swayed gently, as if in a breeze, and caught the light, splitting it into rainbows. There was something a little odd about it, as if its edges were not quite lined up with the space it was in. As he approached it, he felt his skin prick a little, as if he were near something electric. He moved away from it gratefully.

Jack went to sit behind a large desk, on which was a clutter of brass instruments and things that looked like bits of clockwork; there was no computer to be seen.

On the far wall was a rectangular mirror with a gilt frame, and Tom stopped to check himself in the reflection, uncertain whether Zita had come in behind him or not. She had not.

'You do honour to your family, by coming here,' said Jack. 'Great honour. Well pleased I am, my most well-beloved cousin.'

'I don't know...' Tom shifted his weight from his left foot to his right.

Jack scribbled something on a piece of paper, held it up to the light, read it through and then put it on a pile to one side. When he looked up, something flickered behind his eyes, some emotion that Tom couldn't quite grasp. It was like hunger or pity.

Jack cleared his throat. ''Twas a terrible tragedy that happened to your parents. I give you my deepest condolences.'

Tom did not know what to say. He was used to people avoiding the subject or, worse, teasing him.

'Did you ... did you know them?' He picked up a book that was lying on the shelf nearest to him and gazed at the title, unable to make out the words.

'You must have felt great grief.'

It was an understatement. Tom couldn't even begin to describe the gulf that had opened up inside him. Sometimes it was like standing at the edge of a great blackness, a drop that he knew would never end.

Jack, maybe sensing this, said, 'We shall have time enough to talk about them.'

Tom smiled gratefully and placed the book carefully back. 'How long – how long do you want me to stay?'

'As long as you like, my dear boy,' said Jack, laughing. It was a deep laugh. 'As long as you like. You know, I was never blessed with children. I was married once ...'

Jack trailed off, his eyes growing distant, picked up a paperknife and began slicing open some envelopes. It was as if he had suddenly forgotten that Tom was there.

After a moment, in which Jack glanced through some papers and Tom stood awkwardly examining an odd-looking brass ornament that might have been a camel or some kind of horse, Jack focused on Tom.

'Ah. Thomas Swinton. Yes. Go and join the others now, there's a good boy.'

He had just reached the door, when Jack spoke once more. His voice was different, a little flatter.

'Before you go – I would that you do something for me.'

With his hand on the doorknob, Tom turned to look at Jack, who was holding the paperknife point down.

'Sure. I mean, of course.'

'My... domestics. Kit and Zita. You have met them.'

'I... yes, I have,' said Tom, confused.

He slit open another envelope. 'Watch them.'

'That's all?'

'That is all. For now. I shall see you tomorrow. Kit will explain what you must do.'

He went back to his papers, muttering to himself, and Tom closed the door gently behind him.

Chapter 6

18th April, 1846

Sometimes I slip into another place entirely. One that no thinker has ever dreamed of. And then I smell the Suffolk earth, and feel the Suffolk sun on my face, and I am back at home, and Ethel is at the door, telling me the curate is here to see us.

—From the diary of Margaret Ravenswood

Clouds were passing over the afternoon sun, drifting fast. Tom made his way back downstairs through stripes of light and shadow. A smell of chicken stewing and mint and potatoes greeted him as he passed through the hall.

Zita was standing, arms folded, gazing out of the kitchen window. By the kitchen door were racks of boots and oilskin coats. When Tom came in, she half-turned, then dolefully picked up a brush and set to scrubbing a pan.

Kit was cleaning some boots. He coughed. 'You took your time.'

'I was talking to my uncle.'

Tom felt defensive. Who was this strange silver-haired boy?

Were his eyes a genetic abnormality? He'd never heard of anything like it. What was he doing living with his uncle? Was he a friend, a paid help, a servant? And Zita too. How had she ended up here when she seemed a creature of cities and parties?

And why had Jack asked him to watch them? He'd called them his domestics. That meant servants, didn't it? Then that's what they must be. They were always short with each other. A couple, maybe, come to help Jack with the endless tasks of running the farm and the house. No wonder the farm was rundown, if there were only three of them working on it. And Zita hardly looked suited to farm work. Nor, for that matter, did Kit.

Kit put his boots on and stomped towards the kitchen door, where he waited for Tom to come to him. He was clad entirely in black, his silver hair like a halo. He was strikingly handsome, but he didn't seem aware of this fact, looking awkwardly to the side.

'Uncle or no nuncle, you still maun help wi' the work.'

There it was again, that country dialect. The steady ticking of a clock in the kitchen; the chirrup of birds outside. A pair of bluetits fluttered around the branches of a cherry tree, darting back and forth.

Kit took from his pocket a silver chain. On the end of it was not a watch, but a piece of round glass like a lens. He put the glass to his eye and grunted.

'Safe. An' Master's up in his rooms.'

He strode out, before Tom could ask him what he was

doing, and Tom followed. Zita rolled her eyes as he went and flicked a soap sud at him.

The farmhouse was on a little island, surrounded by a moat. A wooden bridge crossed towards the south, where the woods lay; there were a couple of weedy fields. To the north, another bridge led to the path that Tom had come down when he'd arrived.

Tom found, as they crossed the southern bridge, that he was rather surprised to see a large shed, in which he could make out the outline of a tractor. Next to it was some relatively well-kept stabling, and he was pleased to see the head of the black horse poking out, chewing gently.

'So ... what does the farm, you know, farm?' asked Tom as they walked, after he'd gone to stroke the horse between the ears. He didn't know much about the seasons, but he'd have thought that in early summer there might be crops growing, or animals to tend. It was warm, and he was walking quickly to keep up with Kit.

The silver-haired boy did not answer.

Tom looked at his phone; there was no signal. He showed it to Kit, but Kit simply shuddered and turned away.

'What are we doing?' They had reached the western edge of the weedy field nearest the farmhouse.

'We mend a fence.'

A deer had broken through the wire fencing, making a large hole.

Kit set to it, whilst Tom fumbled everything that Kit asked him to do. The silver-haired boy seemed to regard

Tom as an irritant rather than a helper, and soon Tom gave up and just watched him instead.

'An you be so clumsy,' muttered Kit.

He pushed his silver hair away from his face. The wire fence was now fixed, and he leaned on a pole, regarding Tom thoughtfully.

'You've not been bid work a day in your life.'

Tom bridled a little. But he did not take the bait. 'There aren't many wire fences at school.'

Kit sighed. 'Walk wi' me. Now we're walkin' the bounds. Master says you maun do it wi' me once a day, being a Swinton.'

'OK.' Tom found himself falling into step with Kit. 'You call him "Master"?'

He saw in Kit's stance a kind of defiance. But was it to Tom, or was it to James Swinton, Esquire?

From where they stood, the farmhouse looked tiny and exposed. He blinked, and a strange thing happened. The air around the house shimmered and shifted, and he saw for a moment what seemed like an entirely different house, filling out with towers and crenellations; but it was only there for less than a heartbeat, and then it was gone.

'Did you ... ?' But Kit was already several feet away. He blinked again, and the farmhouse was as it had been when he arrived, rambling and tumbledown, a chimney smoking.

What had he seen? It must have been a trick of the sun and the shadows.

42

A faint thumping sound was coming from somewhere, and when Tom looked at him with an enquiring expression, Kit simply said, 'Bird scarers,' and walked onwards.

The farmlands were not large, comprising a few scrubby fields. Even Tom could tell that no crops had grown in them for a long time. No sheep grazed and no other horse poked its head over a fence, looking for an apple or a friendly hand. Sometimes a hare would flash across the field, and Kit would stiffen and look after it, as though he wanted to shoot it for the pot. Tom was pleased to see a hedgehog, snuffling along; it paused and regarded them with interest, before curling up into a ball.

They continued to walk the bounds. Every so often Kit would bring out the chain with the glass on the end of it, stop and hold it up to his eye. Once Tom tried to grab it, but Kit held it out of his reach, and Tom didn't press the point, though he was curious as to what he was doing.

They stopped at the juncture of two grassy foot-paths. A large oak tree shaded them; the hedgerows were alive with birdsong. In a field beyond, a red kite swooped. Somewhere far distant were the noises of car engines.

Kit looked through the glass and grunted. Then he said, 'Close your eyes an' take my hand.'

Tom folded his arms.

'Do as I say.'

Shrugging, Tom took Kit's right hand and closed his eyes.

Kit murmured some words in a language that Tom didn't understand.

43

'Go to it. Say it wi' me.'

'What are we doing? Is this some kind of game?'

'Just do it.'

Kit was clutching the chain, his knuckles whitening. There was something both pleading and commanding in his tone. *Well*, thought Tom, *what's the worst that can happen?* Tom repeated the syllables, not understanding them.

Suddenly, once more, he felt as if reality were sliding away from him. The solid world began to shiver, and he wondered briefly if he had been drugged that morning. He glanced at Kit, but Kit was still muttering the words, eyes tightly shut.

Tom closed his eyes. Now he saw a shimmering wall of light and energy enclosing the entire farmlands. It was astonishing. Power was crackling off it. The words, he saw, were taking on power and life of their own, weaving into the walls, and feeding into them.

He felt a spasm in his stomach, and watched his own power flow out, in a river of light, and falter, and then come up against something that sent it curling back to him. It hit him with a punch.

'Folk been there,' said Kit. 'Hold steady.'

He tried again; and this time, Tom realised he could avoid the obstruction, and weave round it. Now he could not stop saying the words, could not break what he was doing, knowing that if he did, he would end something vital. He explored along the length of the wall. At various points it was weak, as if animals had been making inroads into it, and at other points it was thick and strong. The words

44

were bound up with the wall, and fed themselves into the scheme of it.

Kit kept repeating the words, harsh syllables with deep meanings Tom could almost grasp, and Tom followed him, getting stronger and stronger, until he and Kit were evenly matched. As their voices joined together, there was a sudden burst of light and the whole wall glowed with renewed energy.

Then Tom had to let Kit's hand drop. He gasped, opening his eyes. Someone was walking their dog a few fields away. A bee was lazily hovering near his nose. He stumbled, grasping onto a tree trunk for support. Kit regarded him with an unreadable expression.

'What happened?' said Tom, when he had recovered.

'Master was right. You don' need no training.' He spoke thickly, and Tom couldn't tell if he was praising him or damning him.

'What's going on – what is this? Did you drug me?' It couldn't be happening, thought Tom. This was impossible. A house that changed as he looked at it, walls of energy surrounding them.

'Them's the wards. We keep them up. We don' let the Folk in. Shalt find out soon enough,' answered Kit.

'I'm not going any further till you tell me. Who are they? The Folk? Are they the same people that shot that arrow at us?'

Infuriatingly, Kit chewed slowly on the end of his nail and then spat out of the side of his mouth. 'Master'll tell you soon enough.'

He strode on and Tom, flummoxed, scampered after him.

They stopped at another junction. There was a drained feeling in Tom's limbs. Kit grabbed Tom's hand once more.

'We have to do it again? I don't … I don't think I can …'

'You maun!' Kit spoke savagely, more savagely than Tom had heard him yet, and he was reminded of Zita's snarl. *Watch them*, Jack had said. Was this what he meant?

'And if I don't?'

Kit said, after a deep sigh, 'Folk'll get in.'

Tom thought of the arrow, quivering, an inch away from him. The beat of the bird scarers.

Kit grasped Tom by the wrist. Once more there was that plaintiveness, deep in his silver eyes.

'All right,' said Tom. Kit released him, and Tom felt the place where he'd gripped. It hurt a little.

Sweat was pooling down his neck. He didn't understand; he didn't know what was happening to him. Only a day or so ago he had known, or thought he'd known, the limits of his world. *But I was wrong*, he thought. *I was wrong.*

And so, gently at first, they repeated the process. They did it at crossroads, at the corners of fields, several times, and each time Tom found it easier to find and avoid the strange dark points of the Folk's power; although as he said the words, he felt power pouring out of him until his bones ached.

'When can we stop?' he said, after they'd done it four times. But Kit simply pressed onwards, and Tom had no choice but to follow.

Once, Kit paused by an ash tree, and Tom wondered if he was also tired. Kit closed his eyes and muttered something. Tom noted this in a half-aware kind of way and wondered if it was the sort of thing that Jack was going to ask him about. He didn't feel comfortable watching Kit, even if he was up to something.

By the time they had reached the small pond on the south-western side of the farm, he was beginning to droop, his movements languid.

Kit was a silent companion, only speaking the words of the wards when he needed to do so, but he did not seem to be affected in the same way. Perhaps he had unusual reserves of power. He did, however, offer Tom some water from a leather flask and an apple as they walked, and Tom took them gratefully, enjoying the crisp freshness of the fruit and the coolness of the water more than he ever had.

He checked his phone, feeling the compulsion to connect to someone else, to text Fred, scroll through the social media sites. Kit flinched when he saw the phone.

'I bid you – put that away.'

'"I bid you"? Is that some Suffolk thing?'

Kit grimaced, and Tom shoved the phone back into his pocket, where it made an uncomfortable bump against his thigh.

There was still no signal. The only high ground he could see was the mound in the centre of the wood. He decided to go and visit it soon, picturing himself standing there in the sun on his tiptoes, squinting, stretching his phone up into the air.

As they returned to the farmhouse, which lay as if crouching on the island, he felt completely exhausted. It was about half past four. He thought he could eat a whole loaf of bread.

Drinking a mug of tea by the range and swallowing down some hot toast, he thought he might email Fred and his guardian and Fletch, and said, 'I don't suppose you have WiFi here?'

Kit grunted.

'A dial-up modem?' He sipped deeply from his mug. Surely that was possible, even out here in the sticks.

But Kit simply left Tom alone in the kitchen with only a curt instruction not to bother the Master.

There was only the ticking of the clock and the sound of the birds.

When he'd finished his tea and found a chocolate biscuit, he wandered through the farmhouse. Though it appeared completely deserted, he half-hoped he might run into his uncle. He wanted to see more of Jack's rooms and the strange things in them, and to ask him about the wards and his parents. He wondered idly where Zita might be.

The ground floor was very sparse. There was the kitchen, with its old range; this was fairly well kept, being at least free of the dust and cobwebs that seemed almost an intrinsic part of the rest of the house.

The entrance hall was the main room on the ground floor. There was a tattered leather armchair by the fireplace, a lit lamp on a round table beside it, some tapestried straight-backed chairs and a largeish window looking out onto the bridge and the wood. The candles still stood in a line, now blown out. Bookcases occupied either side of the fireplace, full of leather-covered volumes. Some of them appeared to be in languages that Tom had never seen or heard of.

A painting hung over the fireplace, grimed and cracked with age, of a dark-browed man in an Elizabethan ruff. Tom thought he looked a bit pained by the ruff, but perhaps that was the expression of all portraits of a certain age. His eyes, at least, were wise and kind. Beneath it was a carefully polished brass plaque that said, in calligraphic writing

> Wm. Swinton, Gent. 1503-1560
> *hanc domum aedificavit*
>
> William Swinton, Gentleman
> He built this house

On a semi-circular table by the door were some papers, including, Tom noted with surprise, a prospectus for Downshire College from some years ago and a few official-looking letters.

There were two smaller storerooms coming off it, filled with candles and buckets and so forth, and a door leading down into a cellar. He edged it open, and immediately decided not to go in there. The stairs were steep, and it looked and smelled damp.

The sitting room, which was next to the kitchen, had two comfortable-looking armchairs in it and some cushions and rugs; but it was deserted and it looked as if nobody really used it; there was another small boxroom next to it, in which something scuttled. Tom shut the door quickly.

A flight of higgledy-piggledy stairs led up. He paused at the bottom, listening, then climbed two steps at a time. The first floor, where his room was, was a confusing ramble of corridors uneven in height: some rooms came off the central corridor; others seemed to exist in places where there couldn't be rooms, down little nooks and alcoves.

He found, three doors down from his own bedroom, what was obviously a library, full, like Jack's rooms, of bookcases that spilled over with volumes, most of which were battered from heavy use.

He scanned around for a table with a phone on it, expecting to see something old-fashioned, with dial-up numbers, or even like the phones he'd seen in ancient black-and-white films, where you spoke into a tube. There was nothing. 'Guess there's no computer hiding in here either,' he said to himself, poking about in some cupboards. They were just full of more books and manuscripts. 'Not even a typewriter.' He picked up one of the books at random. It seemed to be a list of local worthies from the seventeenth century. Edward Grist, JP. Salathiel Shingles, MP. 'Not much use,' he murmured, glancing down the names, and noting a James Swinton there, listed as 'Gent., Mundham Farm'.

When he put the book back, he looked up at the wall, which contained many portraits. There was one of a James Swinton, who must, looking at the dates, Tom surmised, have been William's son. Here he saw a resemblance to his own father in his younger days; he moved quickly on.

Then there were some men and women in the elaborate dress of the eighteenth century; a couple of rather dandyish ones from the nineteenth; and then photographs of sombre men and ladies in black and white.

Tom recognised his grandfather and grandmother, posed formally. Underneath was a photograph of Tom with his own parents, showing him standing, smiling. He did not recognise the background, which seemed to be a park; but he did recognise the dress his mother was wearing, red with yellow polka dots, and his father in an open white shirt and ironed cream slacks.

He wondered how James had acquired it. Had his mother and father sent it to him? Had they known this James? Tom didn't think it possible. He didn't remember them sending cards to any James Swinton at Christmas.

From somewhere he thought he could hear gentle music playing; it was probably Zita, shut up in her room.

What was he doing here? He'd come because of a letter, because of the boy that had brought a letter to him, because of the warning that strange man had given him. But was this freedom?

He looked out of the window onto the lawn below, which was sprouting weeds. The lurcher was sniffing at something near the moat; but otherwise there was nobody in sight. What was he getting into? He looked around the library, the dust, the boring books.

This was ridiculous. He would go back to school, and face Fletch. He would be able to find a way to deal with him. He'd be able to get into the town and return to normal life, whatever that was.

He managed to find his room and began throwing things into his so recently unpacked bag.

He had just zipped it up when the door opened. Zita was poised in the frame. She didn't comment on the bag, but her lip curled and her eyes narrowed.

Tom deflated immediately.

'Thinking of skipping the joint?' she said, slowly unwinding a red silk scarf from around her neck. 'He wants to see you.'

Tom knew that she didn't mean Kit.

Zita sauntered ahead of him a few paces down a corridor he was sure he hadn't noticed before and flung open a thick wooden door.

'In there. Come and find me when you're finished.'

'How …?'

'I'm not easy to miss.'

She all but pushed him through the door, and then he was fully in the room, the door closing behind him.

Silence muffled him. It wasn't the study he'd seen before, book-lined, with that strange glass box or sculpture hanging from the centre. This was a smaller space, more bare, with a couple of tapestried chairs. There was an odd smell, slightly earthy. It was gloomy and overwarm. The fire was lit.

'Zita and Kit.' Uncle Jack spoke from the shadows. He was standing by the fireplace, bolt upright. He smiled at

Tom and bowed, his frail body shaking somewhat. Behind his head was a painting of a young girl in a blue dress feeding grain to a caged songbird. There was a mirror in the cage, and you could see the girl's face in it. 'You will have to suffer them. It is my sincere regret that they are not kinder, but – well. There are reasons,' he added, and then, as if forgetting what he was talking about, turned to look fully at Tom, and Tom was struck again by the grandeur and haggard beauty of his features. A huge bundle of keys rattled at his waist and he clicked them against each other deliberately. 'Observe them, please, as I have asked you to do.'

'You want me to report back on them?' Tom felt a little uncomfortable at his uncle's request.

The old man regarded him beadily. 'You will decide that. Have you perceived anything?'

Uncle Jack went to look out of the window. Tom followed him, and leant against the sill, an arm's length away. Outside the fields stretched.

'Nothing.'

'When you did the wards – was there anything unusual?'

'Oh, nothing. We went round.' Tom didn't know what to say. Then he remembered. 'Kit stopped once.'

'He did, did he? Where did he stop?'

Tom considered. 'I can't quite remember … by a tree.' It didn't feel as if that could be a bad thing to report.

'Well, then.' Jack placed his hands on the stone windowsill and gazed outwards.

'You'll see *them* out there. I have tried to keep them back, all these long years.' He sighed and his weariness was evident. Tom strained, but could only see the leaves of the trees rustling.

'You mean Kit and Zita?'

'No. They are getting closer. Inch by inch. And I am getting weaker.'

'The people who shot the arrow? What Kit calls the "Folk"? Who – who are they?'

Jack sighed and gripped Tom by the shoulder. 'Enemies. Long enemies. It is my duty to keep them out. Only a Swinton can do it. Had my eye on you. The last one. Had my eye on you for a long time.' He coughed and went to a bureau, from which he pulled a roll tied up in a red ribbon. He slipped the ribbon off and rolled it out so that Tom could see.

A genealogy was inked on it. There was Tom's father, William Swinton, with a little crossed pair of swords by his name, which Tom guessed showed he had died. There had been many Swintons branching off in past generations, but Tom's father and grandfather were the only ones in theirs.

Jack took the scroll from him surprisingly gently and rolled it up, leaving Tom feeling as if he had missed something.

'What exactly is it you want me to do?'

'You made the wards, my boy. With Kit. I had hoped for that. And you did well.' He smiled once more, with a great effort, showing uneven, yellowing teeth. 'Many things. Many things, which will become apparent in time, if you listen and learn. For now…' Again he paused, as if uncertain where he was or what he was doing.

Tom trembled a little, looking at his uncle's powerful fingers. Then Jack returned his gaze to Tom once more, his eyes shining with unfathomed depths. 'For now, I wish that you do go to Zita. She shall show you what's what. I'm strong, still.' He patted his chest. 'But it has to be a Swinton. Kit and Zita cannot do it alone.' He coughed and Tom made as if to help him, but Jack held up a hand as if to say, *Do not worry*.

From across the bare floorboards, his uncle Jack looked to Tom like nothing so much as an eagle.

'But what is it?' Tom asked, as firmly as he could manage. 'What is it only a Swinton can do?'

Jack uttered a guttural laugh and coughed into his fist. His britches were a little loose, Tom noticed, and Jack hitched them up. 'Those as are outside. Those as are always outside. Only I have the key to what they want. And it will be your duty to stop them. I am too old now. Too old. Everything is too much. I've had my time. I earned it. It seems odd now.' He expelled a deep sigh. 'I have almost forgotten why I wanted it. But now.' He gestured towards Tom.

'And what if I don't want to do this job?' Tom paced up and down before him, twisting his fingers together.

'You'll want it, boy. You'll want it.'

Tom halted in a patch of warm sunlight.

'Why will I want it?'

There was stillness in the room, as thick as night. 'You'll want it, Thomas, as there isn't anything else. Now be

55

off with you.' He laughed again, and the sound filled Tom's ears. 'We will see each other again.'

Feeling more than a little bewildered, Tom left, and soon found Zita sitting cross-legged on a large red cushion in the middle of the entrance hall. There was a low fire burning, and it gave off a sleepy, sweet scent. Leana was dozing in front of the fire, and she lifted her head slowly, before snuggling back down.

When Zita looked up at Tom, he had a sudden flash of something, as if he'd seen her before.

'Your face,' he said. Then he felt foolish. 'Are you …?'

'A relative of yours, darling? One of the Swintons? Alas, I am not. I'm a … friend of the family. What the French call an *amie de la maison*. You see I was attentive in my lessons. I have been here for … simply ages.' She had a leather pouch beside her, and this she pulled out and offered to him, mimicking the posture of someone he had seen only the day before.

Her profile. Her eyelashes. The shoulders.

With an electric jolt Tom recognised her.

It couldn't be. It was mad.

But then so many mad things had happened already.

'The boy!' he said. 'The boy at school.'

She lifted an eyebrow, as if in triumph.

'How could you have got there? How can it be? Was it – can it be you?'

'In a way,' answered Zita. She resettled herself on her cushion.

'You came to me in the quad. In White Quad, I mean, at school. Yesterday.' He blinked. It really had been only the day before. The boy in the quad, the wild man on the path – all yesterday. He felt suddenly much older. 'I remember, I was sitting on the bench underneath the founder's statue, and I was watching the groundsman picking up litter and thinking about the holidays and my parents. And you came. And went. Between the clock sounding the tenth and eleventh strokes.'

Again she said softly, 'In a way.' Her large, soft eyes blinked at him. Her hair was cut short, in a boyish parting. She pushed back a silver cameo earring that hung against her cheek, and busily picked up a vial of something silvery.

'Now,' she said. 'I'll need your help to get some things. There are draughts I need to make for Jack. Most of the ingredients we can get from the farm or inside the boundaries, but there are some things we need from the woods.'

She hadn't answered his questions. Tom knew she wouldn't. He would have to wait.

'The woods where the enemy live?'

'We have to be careful, obviously. They're not terribly watchful, and they like hunting, and they're not always – here, if you know what I mean, but you still have to be careful. That stunt with the arrow was more of a warning shot, if you will excuse the terrible pun. They won't act on it. You and I will go out in a minute.'

'Look,' said Tom.

Zita, having stood up, stared at him over her shoulder and pouted. She had an amazing ability to discomfit Tom, even without saying anything.

'I need to know. I need to know what's going on here. I've seen so much in the last few hours, I don't even know where to begin.'

'You'll need this,' she said calmly, passing him a scabbard with a short sword in it.

'Are you serious?' he said, holding it clumsily at his waist.

She smirked. 'Well, then. Rather suits you. Have you worn one before?'

The lurcher barked somewhere, and the house, in that way it did sometimes, seemed to shiver, as if it were made of nothing but smoke. The clock in the hallway struck six times.

'What are they – the people outside?' Tom asked.

Zita buckled the scabbard onto a belt for him.

'The people who attacked us!'

Zita yawned, showing her pretty white teeth, and said, 'Darling, don't be such a frightful bore about it. When you've got time, go and have a look in the library. Now be a dear, and adjust this strap for me.'

Chapter 7

20th April, 1846

Papa has begun to ask me where I go to when I am not in the Rectory. He has noticed that I return with twigs in my dress and earth under my fingernails. I told him I was walking in the woods, to contemplate God's beauty in nature. He nodded, and seemed pleased. But he ordered me to go and scrub my hands, and I obeyed.

—From the diary of Margaret Ravenswood

'It's only after you've crossed over the moat that you have to worry,' Zita said as she closed the wooden gate on the bridge behind them.

The early evening sun was moving towards the horizon, but it was still pleasantly warm. The horse was grazing in the field beyond, swatting its tail lazily. Leana lolloped ahead, pausing under a tree, her ears pricked, one paw out as if pointing.

'They can't get over the water, and the wards are meant to stop their magic – but it doesn't always work.'

Magic. It was the first time someone had said that

explicitly. That was what he was dealing with here. That was what he had been doing, making the wards.

'Darling, don't gape so. It makes you look like a fish. Didn't your mother tell you not to gape?' She caught herself and cleared her throat. 'Of course. I had forgotten. I am sorry, old thing.'

'It's fine,' said Tom. He swallowed down the sob that had risen in his throat.

Zita looked him fully in the face. Tom blushed and turned towards the sun. 'If you ever want to talk about it, darling, you've got a friend here. No stiff upper lips necessary. Not any more.'

Tom nodded gratefully. 'Thank you.'

Leana had already shot away and was a small black speck in the distance nearing the woods. In the light behind them, the farmhouse looked inviting, with its warm red brick and a chimney smoking from the fire perpetually burning in the entrance hall.

They reached the wooden gate into the woods. Zita leapt over it without even looking back, and then, before Tom could follow her, unlatched the gate so that he could come through. He gave an ironic bow as he passed her, and she held his gaze mockingly.

Under cover of the trees, the light was more tentative, dappling the forest floor with shadow.

'So you and Kit… are you …?'

'Friends? Of course, darling.' But she did not look into his eyes. 'Kit's been here much longer than I.'

'How did you find the place?' Tom persisted.

'I…' She looked around, as if she couldn't quite remember which direction she had to go in. 'I answered an advert. In *The Lady*, don't you know.'

That fitted with what Tom had thought. He changed the subject, saying how much he was enjoying the sun.

She found the right way. 'We don't have to go far to find what I'm looking for.' Zita strode ahead, her dress billowing out behind her.

Tom wondered how much of the land round about was owned by Jack. They'd walked the bounds in… what? About forty minutes. So it could be a good-sized acreage. The sword at his waist felt ridiculous and he wondered what on earth Zita had given it to him for. He would be absolutely no help in a fight of any sort. And if someone took it and turned it on him… He hurried to catch up with Zita, branches catching at him.

He went over the encounter he'd had with Jack and tried to understand it.

This was not normal. Zita was not normal. The wards were not normal. And yet, this wasn't some weird hippy commune, full of yoga and gurus. This was something else. Quite what it was he had no idea at the moment. One word kept tugging at his mind, and he kept pushing it back, away from him.

Magic.

But there was no such thing, was there?

He could not doubt what he had seen, what he had heard, what he was doing now. What had the wards been, those words, that energy, but magic? What had Zita been doing but magic?

As he walked a few paces behind Zita, he caught sight of a church steeple in the distance, a weathervane on the top of it. There would be people there. If he needed to, he would be able to find someone in the village, someone who had a working phone, and then he would be able to call up Fletch and get back to school.

Zita crouched down at the base of a tree and started to gather some moss with a knife.

'How can you tell the difference between them?' asked Tom. 'They all look the same to me.'

'They all have their signs,' she replied, putting the moss into a bag. 'You gather some too, from that ash tree there. This kind only grows at the bottom of ash trees, for a few weeks in the summer.' She gave him a bag, and he knelt not far from her. The moss smelled sweet, and he began to enjoy the gentle, repetitive movements of cutting and placing in the pouch.

It was very different from making the wards with Kit. That sapped something from inside him; this gave him a new kind of feeling, loamy and rich. He smiled at Zita, and she grinned back: the first time that she did not seem to be loaded with irony.

'When did you learn all of this?'

'I've had plenty of time to do so. Some of it I taught myself. Other things Jack taught me.'

The sun caught her face as she turned to Tom, and he felt a flutter in his chest.

62

A distant yelping pierced the air. Something startled out of the trees. A flash of brown, long ears, twitching whiskers – a hare. And after it, fast as an arrow, Leana.

Zita stiffened and grabbed Tom's arm. The hare was young. The lurcher was almost on it. Tom broke away from Zita and found himself puffing up, with a power he didn't know he had.

'Stop!' The word came out of him like a pistol shot. Dog and hare stiffened and paused, as if held in an invisible web.

Tom reached forwards and grabbed the lurcher by the collar. She strained, retching a little. He wished he'd brought a lead. The young hare, stupefied, turned. Its whiskers trembled, and Leana yanked against Tom's hold. 'Ssh there, shush,' said Tom. Then the hare vanished, almost lazily, back into the woods.

Tom, a smile bursting out of him, laughed with the adrenaline that was coursing through him, and looked to Zita for her to join in.

But instead she was pale and set. She gathered up her things.

'Back now,' she said. 'And quickly.'

Tom, reluctant to let Leana go in case she ran back after the hare, picked her up and half-ran, half-stumbled after Zita, the dog's ungainly body weighing heavy in his arms. He only released her once they had crossed back through the gate and were near the island. She trotted beside him quite peaceably.

Contrary to his promise, Jack did not appear at supper that night. When Tom asked if he should bring up a tray to

63

him in his study, Zita simply snorted. 'He won't be eating anything tonight.'

So Tom, Zita and Kit ate chicken pie, cabbage and potatoes flavoured with mint from the garden, in the kitchen, with candles lit as the sun began to set, drinking fresh clean water. Leana, though, was prowling around the kitchen, ears pricked, scratching at the door moaning to be let out and then not going.

'Something's got into her,' said Tom as he helped Zita wash the dishes in the huge, ancient sink. His supper sat heavily in his stomach. Kit was playing with the glass pendant, letting it spin around and catch the light.

Zita threw a damp tea towel over her shoulder. 'Don't you think I look spiffing? How Moggy Symington would simply seethe to see me now! I never thought I'd spend the rest of my life washing up. So, Tommy,' she said, tapping him lightly with the towel. 'Is there anyone … special in your life?'

Tom thought. 'At school? There aren't any girls.'

'Why should that make a difference? There's plenty of chaps that like one kind or both. Don't look so surprised. I have seen something of the world, you know.'

'No. Nothing like that.' And outside of school, he hardly went to any parties or anything. It was difficult, living in Hector's house in the country, whilst his guardian was away all the time. He'd mostly gone for walks, read or watched endless TV shows.

'You're a handsome chap, you know.'

Tom blushed.

With a theatrical sigh, Zita replaced the tea towel on the cooking range.

Kit coughed. 'You watch her,' he said. It was the clearest thing Tom had yet heard him say.

'Don't listen to him. He's an old stick-in-the-mud.'

Leana's ears pricked up. She was standing with her paws on the windowsill, looking out across the lawn to the bridge.

'Do you dance, darling?' murmured Zita into Tom's ear. She performed a little jig and then bent her knees and bobbed up and down.

'Isn't that a bit old-fashioned?' said Tom. His experience of dancing so far had been at people's sixteenth birthdays, which tended to be mostly in the dark and with music that wasn't anything like this, and where dancing was more a question of throwing yourself around than doing anything that might be called steps. He felt awkward.

'Oh, anyone can do it,' she said. 'Even Kit.'

Kit grunted in reply.

She pulled him by the hand into the hall and lit some candles. There was a gramophone on the floor by the side, and she knelt down and chose a record. Crackly band music boomed around the hall, a trumpet solo dancing up and down the scales. Zita stretched and performed a pirouette, very gracefully. Kit came through and leant against the wall, his silver hair gently shining in the golden light, and the candlelight shone off Zita's black head, her earrings glittering against her white neck. She turned to Tom with a look of infectious naughtiness.

'Come, Tommy dear. Dance. Or should I call you Tom-Tom?'

'Please don't.' Tom found he couldn't help it. She drew him in, and then they were dancing, the music filling Tom in a way he'd never felt before. He stumbled, but Zita didn't seem to mind, and soon he was swaying and stepping in time with her. The lurcher barked, once, and then again. Zita swooned. Kit said, 'Watch it.'

'Quite a dashing young man, really,' said Zita as they danced. 'One would almost think you'd done this before. Do you think Kit's getting jealous?' She leaned in, and Tom felt her breath on his neck.

There was a thundering on the stairs, and Jack was there, filling the room with his presence. The music faltered and crackled. Sighing, Zita drew away from Tom. The old man glared. He seemed entirely different from the person that Tom had spoken to earlier in the day. There was something stronger here.

'Thomas Swinton.'

'Uncle?'

Jack came to the centre of the room, walking tensely, hands clenched. Then he deflated slightly, sighing, as if weighing up things in his mind, and once more he seemed the old man that Tom recognised. 'I am sorry. I did not mean to be so harsh. But in the woods today you did something wrong. I felt it. Know that I will feel things.'

'What did I do?'

'The hare. You let the hare go.'

'I'm sorry.' He must have wanted it for the pot, thought Tom.

'I'm very partial to a jugged hare. Delicious.' It was as if Jack had read his mind, and Tom found himself feeling uneasy.

'I'm sorry,' he said again, uncertain whether he'd broken a rule of the household.

'If it happens again – don't let it get away. But for now I forgive you.' He smiled once more. 'Let us all drink!' He went to the drinks table and, with a trembling hand, poured out four glasses of the dark port. 'And let us dance!

The tension left the room, and Zita turned over the record on the player. The music started up again, and soon Tom and Zita were dancing again, round and round the table, whilst Jack tapped his feet and Kit lurked in the corner and glowered.

Chapter 8

21st April, 1846

There was a storm last night. When I looked out, I saw them riding through the dark. And I thought – he chose me. Of all the people in the village, in the county, in the whole of the world, he chose me.

— From the diary of Margaret Ravenswood

An hour or so had passed, with Kit leaning against the wall whittling something with his knife and Jack sitting quietly in the corner in his tattered armchair turning over the pages of a book, until Tom had almost forgotten that he was there.

It was now fully dark outside.

As Tom and Zita were searching for a new record, Jack suddenly said, 'Kit.'

As if stung by a bee, Kit sprang upright. Tom put the record he was holding onto the player, setting it at a lower volume, and saw that Kit was trembling.

'Nuncle … what be the matter?'

'Kit … dost thou disobey me, boy?'

'Nay, Master …'

Their voices sounded different, more earthy, more countrified. Puzzled, Tom shot a glance at Zita, but she was poised as if about to run from the room.

'What didst thou say? This day, with my kin, what didst thou say, when thou stoodst at the ash tree?'

Kit froze and turned his gaze on Tom.

'Nowt, Master.'

'If thou thinkst thou canst go agin me ...' said Jack softly.

'Nuncle ...'

With a sudden movement like a coiled snake striking, Jack slapped Kit with the back of his hand, leaving the boy sobbing.

Tom leapt up, knowing that somehow he'd made this happen.

'Don't hit him!'

Jack rounded on him, and for the first time, Tom felt afraid. His shadow was long and his body seemed more powerful than before.

'Silence! You know nothing of this.' His voice returned to its usual tone. 'Remember, you're a Swinton, remember that.'

He grabbed Tom's arm and pressed it with his forefingers, holding him with surprising strength. Tom was now up close to him, and he saw a deep, dark fury in his eyes that he had not noted before. He found he could not move.

Release came from an unexpected corner. In her cocktail dress, her pearls glinting, Zita rounded on Jack, full of fury.

'He's not you, old man!'

A saxophone blared out from the gramophone. The needle stuck, the same note repeating again and again.

69

Jack closed his eyes and muttered. Tom watched, aghast, as something that looked like smoke issued from his fingers and, floating, oozed across the room in a rope, winding itself round Zita's wrist, solidifying into a silver bracelet.

'You old fool!' she snarled. Then she gasped with pain. The bracelet was digging into her flesh. 'You know I can get this off, *darling*,' she hissed.

'Try it then!' Jack roared.

Zita, tossing her head back, swooped off to her room.

Kit simply stood with his back to the stone wall, limp, like a puppet. *The silver*, thought Tom. *The silver is the same as in Kit's eyes and his hair. What did Jack do to him? What did he do to deserve this? What kind of punishment is he suffering?*

Jack released Tom and slumped into the armchair. His eyes were alight.

'Tomorrow,' he wheezed at Tom, 'you shall go with him. And watch him. Leave her alone. She'll stew. Kit! Pour me a drink.'

Without looking at Tom, Kit scurried to a side table and served Jack a glass full of wine, which the old man took and drank from deeply, smacking his lips. And then he motioned to Kit with a long finger and suggested that he should give Tom a drink as well. As he sat in the shadows, Tom couldn't help but be reminded of the large spider he'd seen on the landing.

'I'm tired… I… think I'll go to bed.' Tom backed away, and then leapt up the stairs to his room, two at a time, and slumped down with his back to the door, huddled in a patch of moonlight.

70

That night, all Tom's thoughts were bent on leaving Mundham Farm. Jack. His uncle. Who was he? He no longer seemed an old eccentric, but someone alarming. What was he doing to Kit and Zita? What might he do to Tom? He hardly slept, imagining the red-brick farmhouse shivering on its foundations. He was more grateful than ever for the lurcher, who had crept in and slept on his bed at his feet, occasionally lifting her graceful head at some noise.

He would leave in the morning, he decided. He would have to call a taxi. Maybe there would be reception on the top of the mound. He'd spotted the scarlet livery of an old phone box on the drive in from the station, probably about twenty minutes' walk away, by the side of the road. Might it still be in use? He had some change in his bag, from buying breakfast at Liverpool Street Station.

What had been the name of the taxi company? Ben's Taxis, that was it. He could call it and have it meet him at the bottom of the drive. He fantasised about saddling up the horse and riding out.

Eventually, he slept, his sleep bleeding into dreams. In them he wandered the corridors of the house. Some were familiar, some were not. They twisted and turned out of his reach, sometimes opening into rooms that could not be there, full of secrets and shadows, and in the middle of all the dreams was a wooden chest that somehow was in all of the rooms at once and in none of them. Light and music poured out of it, dizzying and wonderful, and the music and the light enveloped him in warmth.

When he woke the next morning, he longed for them again.

Entering the kitchen, yawning, some time past nine o'clock the next day, Tom saw that breakfast was under way. Kit was already there, wearing his customary black, laying crockery on the table. Leana was snuffling about on the scrubby lawn outside, and the horse was out in the field. No trace of Zita, apart from a discarded silver scarf lying across a chair. And, fortunately, no sign of Jack. Tom poured himself a cup of tea from the pot on the table.

The first thing Tom wanted to do was apologise. Kit did not acknowledge him, but Tom touched him gently on the shoulder. The boy shuddered away.

'Look, Kit, I'm sorry. I didn't know what I was doing.'

'You be his kin,' said Kit gently. 'Your bond be to him.'

Tom felt a stab of guilt in his gut. 'I didn't mean to tell on you – I don't know what you were doing. I don't care. I'm not his spy.'

Kit turned away and bent over the porridge pot. From upstairs there were rumbles, as if Zita were stomping round her room.

The bird scarers that he had heard the day before were going already. Insistent, thumping.

'I'm not here to watch you, I promise.'

But Kit just ladled a bowl of porridge for himself and tilted his chin in the direction of the table.

A few minutes later, Jack stalked in. The atmosphere thickened. Tom saw Kit's shoulders tense. There was an

72

array of decanters on a tray on the sideboard, and Jack opened one and poured out a small measure of dark wine, indicating to Tom that he should have one too.

'Well rested, are you?'

Tom nodded and took a deep gulp of his tea.

'You won't have a drink?'

'Tea … tea's what I usually have in the morning.'

'No? No, well, I will have it on my own.' He smiled darkly and took the wine in one go.

The last remnant of Tom's family, standing in front of him, swigging port wine. Once again he saw his father's face in the angles of Jack's, and it caused an ache in his stomach.

A sudden high-pitched noise came from outside. Jack looked up, startled, and an ugly grimace passed over his face.

Kit dropped the cloth he was carrying and ran to the window, saying, 'I did not hear him, Master.' Tom joined him. 'I did not feel him.' He pulled the chain from his pocket and held the glass pendant up to his eye. 'I cannot see him here.'

'They must have learnt of your device. We will have to find some other way of seeing them.'

A dark figure, cloaked, was standing on the other side of the moat.

'Master …' said Kit. 'By the bridge …'

'I can see, Kit. I can see well enough.' Jack's voice was level, but full of something that threatened to spill out into fury. 'How dare he come to the bridge!'

'Who is it? The one who shot at us?' Tom's voice shook.

'One of them. One of the Samdhya. I do not recognise him.'

73

The Samdhya lifted a hand. A ball of burning light formed in it.

'He has broken the wards! Was this your work, Kit, at the ash tree?'

'Nay, Master, nay!'

Grinning, the Samdhya hurled the ball of light towards the house. They watched it sear through the air like a comet.

Kit gasped as if he had been hit in the stomach, and there was a shattering sound. They rushed through the door, Jack moving surprisingly fast.

In the hall, shards of glass were scattering. The entire window had blown inwards.

Jack stormed to the gap, heedless of the jagged fragments. 'He broke through.' He bent down with savage power and picked up the shimmering ball of flame where it lay smoking on the flags. 'He broke through the wards.' The flames did not seem to harm him, but licked around his forearms as if he were made of stone.

'Take heed, James Swinton,' called the Samdhya, now uncloaking himself, the red lining billowing out in the breeze, long black hair flaming behind him. 'Take heed, you and your whelp.'

Tom saw the leopard tattooed on his face. It was him, the one who had warned him, the one who had cut him behind the school. He should have listened to him.

Jack gathered himself together and sent the blazing stone flying back out of the window. 'Shalt see!' he shouted. 'After the hour of noon, shalt see what thou hast wrought!'

74

The effort left him gasping, clutching the back of a tapestried chair.

It had worked. The missile was soaring over the moat and slammed straight into the Samdhya, shoving him over onto his back.

Kit's eyes were closed; his hands were tightly clenched and his brow furrowed. Tom watched in astonishment as he muttered a word, and the glass on the ground shivered, before rising up and fitting itself back together into the window.

When it had finished, Jack, still smouldering with rage, shook his fist; but the Samdhya had gone. A thin spiral of smoke was all that remained.

Exhausted, Kit sank to the floor and put his head in his hands.

'Well, Tom,' said Zita, who had appeared and was standing at the bottom of the stairs. The silver bracelet was still on her wrist; it puckered her skin. 'I suppose you've properly met your first Samdhya now. Charming, aren't they? Such a way with words.' She twirled round, her dress glittering. 'And so elegant. They always make me want to dance.'

'Stop it, Zita,' gasped Kit. 'I need your healing draught.'

'What happened?'

'Had to put the window back…'

'Oh you poor thing. You must be shattered. Oh, dear, there I go again. I didn't mean to pun.' Genuinely perturbed, Zita rushed to the kitchen and reappeared a few seconds later with a mug full of hot water, into which she was

75

pouring some thick, dark liquid. 'Here. This will restore you.' She stirred it with a spoon and handed it to him.

Kit took it, sipped and then swallowed the mixture. He gagged, but almost immediately, colour returned to his face. He relaxed a little.

All the while, Jack was striding up and down, muttering, 'He broke through the wards. We could not see him. He has discovered some new way, some new path. I must find it out, I must.'

'Tell me.' Tom gripped the windowsill. 'Tell me what's going on. I saw one of them at school. He told me to stay there and not to disturb the past. Why? Why would he want me not to come here?'

'You've seen one before?' Zita glanced at Jack, who paused and nodded slightly. She yawned and patted her mouth in an arch manner. 'Well now, how long have you got? Oh, silly me, you're not going anywhere. Come up to my room and I'll tell you.'

Kit said, 'He maun do the rounds. We maun strengthen the wards.'

Jack grunted. It was clear to Tom that both Kit and Zita were in thrall to him.

'Well, if you must, darling,' said Zita, drawing herself up. 'But don't keep him all to yourself, will you?' Kit reddened, all the way down his neck. She grabbed the front of Tom's shirt at the neck and said, 'Come straight up afterwards.'

They got ready to walk the bounds. Jack disappeared back to his rooms. The glass pendant which Kit had been using

76

to see the Samdhya was now useless. Kit hung it carefully on a hook in the kitchen.

It was ten o'clock. Outside, the land looked drained and grey, the sky washed out, the sun shining feebly through a thick mantle of cloud. Even the horse in his field seemed quiet, staying close to the fencing and his stable.

Walking itself was difficult, as if they were wading through mud. There was no sign of any movement. There were few birds. Leana did not come with them, and Tom wished for her gentle company. He noticed the drabness of the land around even more keenly, how no flowers grew.

This time, as they walked the bounds, Tom could interpret Kit's laconic commands more easily, and he found that the wards came faster. When he held Kit's hand and closed his eyes, again he saw the silver wall, pulsing with strange, dark energy. There was now a hole in it. And as he spoke with Kit, he added his own, new words, sounds which came to him from somewhere he did not know, and he was able to pour some of his own self into the space which had been broken.

He knew that when he finished it was stronger than it had been before, stronger than it had ever been, perhaps. When he felt along the silver wall, he could somehow trace back the power. He could feel Kit there and Jack and some other threads that he knew were Zita's. But her power was of a different sort, warmer and loamier. Kit's was hard and cold. And as for Jack's – it was wild and strange and terrifying, and when Tom touched it, he drew away as fast as he was able to.

When they finished the wards, ending as usual by the pond, and came tramping up the weed-strewn drive to the front door, Kit even gave Tom a little grudging nod as he went back in, as if to say, *You did well.* When Kit looked into his eyes Tom felt an unexpected rush of warmth.

Kit disappeared into the recesses of the house, and Tom, after he'd restored himself with some biscuits and tea, went to find Zita.

Her room was along the corridor from his, next to the library. It was much larger, taking up seemingly about half of the house, with one large window facing onto the lawn, and several small windows set high up into the ceiling; and bursting with clothes that hung or were draped everywhere over furniture, and books that had obviously come from the library.

'I've read everything at least twice,' she sighed. 'You wouldn't believe how fascinating these old accounts of cattle shows can become. Fortunately, there's a relatively large collection of the playwrights. But I have read *Hamlet* about four hundred times now. Plenty of the classics, naturally, so my Latin's a lot better than it used to be. Jack barely reads anything himself now, of course. Too busy... brooding. Cocktail?' She offered him a tall glass, in which was a clear liquid, a large ice cube and some shining red berries. Tom demurred. 'Don't be shy, darling, it's only vodka. And the berries won't kill you, I promise.'

'Kill me? Or send me insane ...?'

'Or do anything else. Honestly, look at you, you're like a frightened rabbit. How one wants to pick you up and murmur sweet comforts into your ear.' She smoothed down her skirt. 'I had a rabbit when I was a girl.'

'What happened to it?'

'Monsieur Snuffles, I called him, because he looked French.'

'Did he die happily, surrounded by all his grieving rabbit descendants?'

Zita wrinkled her nose. 'Eaten by a fox, of course.'

She went to a pile of books and picked one that lay on the top. It was a journal, bound in red boards, with the initials M.H.R. on the front. 'Here,' she said, 'is a good place to start. This is the diary of the daughter of a local rector in the late nineteenth century. She was rather a bright spark, don't you know, and she met one of the Samdhya and kept detailed notes. Margaret Ravenswood her name was.'

Tom took the book. *Will this help me understand?* he thought. He flicked open the front cover and then looked up at Zita. 'Your wrist…' he said. 'Kit's eyes… his hair… the silver…'

'Careful now, Tommy boy,' whispered Zita.

'It comes from Jack, doesn't it? I know it. The wards around the house, it's all him, it's all connected. What is he? What is he doing?'

Zita blew out her cheeks, rustling her fringe, and delicately ate a red berry. Then, when she saw that Tom would not be put off, she said, 'There is a storm, you see. A storm in the world, and Jack is at the centre of it. James Swinton, Esquire, has something that belongs to the Samdhya, and they want it. They think that because you are of his blood you are going to help him and keep it all locked up, and they will never be able to get it back. They haven't dared to attack fully – they know what will happen if they do. Watch what happens today.'

'What will happen?' asked Tom.

For once, the light expression left Zita's eyes, replaced by a look of deep sorrow. 'Oh, Tom.' She touched his hand, gently and then withdrew it quickly.

'What does he have? I don't understand.'

Zita sipped her drink, touching her teeth with her tongue briefly. 'One of them, Tom. He's got one of them, captured.'

'One of the Samdhya? Why? What for?'

'It will come to you, after all.' Zita stood and brushed down her red dress. She adjusted the scarf around her neck. 'It's important to look elegant, don't you think? Even despite it all.'

'You're not answering my question.'

'Wouldn't we all want it? Wouldn't you want it?' Tapping her slender white fingers against the sides of her glass, she sighed. 'Life, Tommy boy. Life. Life that lasts for as long as the Samdhya. As long as the sun and the moon.'

She went back to the pile of books, took a heavier tome up and passed it to him. It was a ledger, open at a particular page which had been marked down with a leather bookmark.

It was a parish register, inked in careful writing, faded now with age. She placed a finger under a name, then read it out.

'Here we are. James Swinton. Father, William Swinton, gentleman. Mother, Anne Greenwood, daughter of Thomas Greenwood, worsted weaver. Place of birth, Mundham, Suffolk. Date of birth: fourteenth of March, in the year of our Lord, 1543.'

'An ancestor,' said Tom. 'My ancestor. My father's ancestor.'

Outside, the bird scarers. Inside, Zita's gentle breath, her head bent towards him. Tom calculated. His thoughts whirled.

'Perhaps that's enough for today.' Zita raised her eyebrows and closed the ledger, placing it gently down on a pile, and took a long swig of her drink, so that the ice tinkled against the sides of the glass.

The house seemed to bend and shift around Tom. He clutched onto a beam for support and then felt his knees trembling. 'The drink – did you put something in it?'

'Absolutely not, darling.' Zita shook her head. 'It's a lot to grasp.'

Jack, ancient, gauntly beautiful, hurling a ball of fire through a window. Jack, James Swinton, but several hundred years old. 'Not my uncle at all. It can't be true.'

'You've seen a lot already, Tommy boy. Why not believe this too?'

There was a sound outside on the lawn, a brief shout and a rustling, hissing noise.

'Right on time. Always a stickler for punctuality, Jack Swinton. Now,' she said, 'come with me and look out onto the lawn and you'll see.'

They leant on the windowsill and peered down through the glass. Tom was still reeling from his new knowledge, as it flowed through him like wine, making him giddy and sick.

Jack was standing there on the lawn, and someone was with him. Someone Tom had not seen before, tall and longer than a human, with long, dark plaited hair, wearing a long black fur around her neck and a white robe embroidered with silver. She looked ill and pale, her cheeks hollow, her eyes sunken. Iron manacles were clasped around her hands and feet, joined with heavy silver chains.

Though he could see nobody else outside, Tom had the sense that a hundred eyes were watching, from trees, from bushes. Something flashed in the forest – a hare, perhaps, darting away, or a deer.

Jack pushed the prisoner down onto her knees and held up a jagged iron bar. He brandished it, holding it out in all four points of the compass, and the trees rustled and stretched their branches.

'See this. See this.' He barked the words twice.

Then, as gently as if he were stroking a dog, he passed the iron bar over the prisoner's arm.

The prisoner screamed and shook bodily, as if she were having a fit, and Jack stood triumphant. For a moment Tom saw, instead of trees and bushes, hundreds of tall warriors, all watching, all armed with bows and arrows, all intent upon this one moment; and then it passed, and Jack had taken the prisoner inside, and the lawn and the fields and the trees were empty.

'You see,' said Zita. 'You see. The iron. They can't abide it. Never could. It hurts them, like fire would hurt us, like poison. He's got them where he wants them. They can't cross over the moat, and it's almost impossible for them to break the wards. But sometimes … they can.'

'Why did you stay? Why *do* you stay? How can you stay here?' Tom looked wildly around the room. 'We'll go, today, this evening, when he's asleep, we have to go, we have to.'

The silver bracelet on her arm was digging into her skin. Zita brushed her hair away from her face.

'You try to leave, darling,' she whispered, looking up at him with her gentle, shining eyes. 'Just you try.'

Chapter 9

1st June, 1846

He has been gone now for ten days. I watch for him every night, and I do not see him in the moonlight by the ash tree. The hours stretch out before me, empty. I do not know what to do with myself. My father thinks I am pining for Horace the curate. I do not disabuse him of this notion. He eats his eggs with relish in the morning, thinking that soon I am to marry, and that one of his troublesome daughters will be safely provided for. He has started to write the sermon he will give. I hear him practising it under his breath.

— From the diary of Margaret Ravenswood

The morning after he'd seen the prisoner on the lawn, Tom was sitting slumped in the window seat of the library. It was another grey day, the sun gleaming weakly off the surface of the moat. Just below, he could see the dark shapes of fish, weaving about; something must have disturbed them, because they scattered.

The night before he had dreamed, and he hadn't known if he was dreaming or not, so vivid had it been. He'd been falling through a great darkness, through a square inside a square inside another, until he reached the smallest square of all. And inside that there was nothing, nothing at all.

Now his knees were drawn up to his chin and he was looking out across the island and the moat towards the mound where it loomed up from the trees.

As far as Tom could tell, Jack never went out of the house.

Tom could hear him now, stomping about in his rooms.

Two paths lay in front of Tom. He could try to leave. But what might Jack do to him? Would he hurt his own flesh and blood? Would he cast a glamour on Tom and turn his hair and his eyes silver? Kit was so far in Jack's power now, he was barely his own person. The bracelet around Zita's wrist – that was a way of controlling her, Tom could see that. And Zita. Could he leave her here, becoming ever more like Kit? He couldn't imagine Zita without that ironic gleam in her eyes, that flamboyant warmth.

Or he could stay and find the Captive and release her, and Zita too, and Kit.

And then what might happen? Could he face Jack and the strange, dark powers he had at his command?

And that was not the only threat. What would happen to him if the Samdhya broke through the wards and poured into the house?

But they could not cross the moat, he reminded himself. Then perhaps he would have to remain in the house until his own death, a different kind of prisoner.

There was a third path. Could Jack make him his own, give him the gift of eternal life? Was that something that Tom even wanted? To become like Jack, to have control of things beyond the knowledge of any, living as a darker shadow among shadows.

The lurcher appeared at the door and regarded him inquisitively with her bright black eyes. She was a welcome appearance. 'I know what you want,' said Tom and swung himself down onto the ground.

Kit had said it was safe to go out into the woods: the Samdhya wouldn't try anything for a while, not after what they'd seen Jack do. They always retreated when they'd pushed him too far. That was why they would never properly attack the house. They knew the pain it would cause the Captive.

Tom was glad to leave the oppressive mustiness of the farmhouse. Zita was in her room, listening to records, and Kit was tending to the vegetable patch, weeding methodically. Tom raised a hand in greeting, and the boy simply nodded back. As he crossed the north bridge, he turned and saw someone flash past a window, but whether it was Jack or Zita he could not tell.

He did not care if Jack saw him go. Or at least, that is what he told himself.

There was in his mind half an idea to check the bounds by himself and see if he could find another way out of the farm's land which didn't mean going straight down the drive or over the fields in front of the house.

His geography was hazy, but he knew that Suffolk was mainly flat; there was the church steeple to the north, and there must, he surmised, be more villages or hamlets around. If he needed to, he could run in any direction and find somewhere. They were not that far from civilisation, though at times it seemed as if they were entirely sealed off.

He remembered Zita's apparition at school. Jack had known he was at Downshire; Tom had seen the prospectus himself on the table. But would Jack be able to locate him? How far did his powers and his abilities reach? Would he be able to send Zita after him and bring him back somehow? Could Jack do similar things? The thought of encountering some wraith-like version of Jack made him shudder.

Through dappled light he walked; the church steeple appeared through the tops of the trees, and he realised he was a lot closer to it than he'd thought. The edge of the wood in fact bordered onto the graveyard. Mossy statues of angels and crumbling headstones peeked over a wall on the verge of tumbling down. Tom, fearing to lean on it, looked over, but could not see any sign of movement or habitation in the church. Perhaps it was empty; perhaps nobody had worshipped there for centuries. He could make out some names on the gravestones. There was a William Swinton, almost rubbed away with age, lichen covering half the stone.

The lurcher came to his heel and regarded him inquisitively. Her intelligent eyes seemed to beckon him onwards, and she jumped up at him, placing her paws on his arm. 'All right then, you. Off we go.' He turned towards the path that would lead deeper into the woods, and breathed in the soft air. It was fresh and it was beautiful.

Something twanged, and a black-fletched arrow stuck into the ground at his feet.

Terrified, he looked up, to see, standing in the middle of the path, facing him, bow in hand, flowers woven into her hair, a girl.

She had a mocking smile on her lips. The lurcher whined and hid behind Tom's legs. She was tall, taller than Tom by half a head or so. Her nostrils twitched, and she moved with animal urgency.

'Do not be afraid. My fellows are away, seeking the Knot. They would be angry if they knew I was here.' Like the Samdhya he'd met at school, her accent was hard to place; guttural, almost as if she found the words hard to say.

And yet there was an edge of familiarity about it, reminding Tom of something far off in his memory, some voice, some face.

Tom stuttered and backed away. As if realising something, she carefully placed her bow on the ground. She took the quiver off her back and laid it down in the long grass beside the bow. Around them the breeze rustled through the leaves, and a muntjac barked nearby.

He should run, thought Tom. But she would catch him. 'The arrow,' said Tom. 'In the cart, when I arrived. It nearly got my hand.'

'It was a warning.'

Tom was only a foot away from her. Leana kept close to his legs.

The girl was wearing a wine-coloured tunic and dark jewels shone around her neck. They seemed to shift colour as he watched. She had a tattoo on her cheek – a tattoo he had seen before.

'The one that Jack has. She made the flowers come. Blue and white. That's when the balance was true. Jack has upset the balance.'

'Who would be angry with you?' Tom managed to say, not understanding what she said.

'They would. My companions. My brothers and sisters. The Storm, the Deep. The Wildmark. Because I have come to thank you.'

Mystified, Tom said, 'I'm sorry, I don't – I don't know what you mean.'

She laughed and knelt, holding her hand out for the dog to sniff. A buzzard mewed. After a second or two, the lurcher padded forwards and licked her hand.

'She will not chase me now.' She looked up, as if she had heard distant voices. The deer barked once more, insistent and loud. 'I must go, or they will know.' She sprang up, agile and lithe, and then she was gone, melted into the trees like a doe.

Tom felt as if he had been in contact with something wild – a fox or a stoat or an owl. He looked around, desperate to catch sight of her again.

In her place, on the grassy path, was a small wooden flute. There was a carved hare on the end of it.

Tom placed it carefully in his pocket. The lurcher sprang after a squirrel, which scuttled up a tree, and Tom turned his steps back to the farm.

It was a message. A clear message. He held the flute tightly and wondered what would happen if he played it. Would it summon something? Might it summon her? She had made it, and he felt the wood beneath his fingers, knowing she had touched it and crafted it and loved it.

He went straight back to his room and hid the flute in his drawer with the photographs and letters from his parents. It still felt warm, as if someone had just stopped playing it.

On his desk was the book that Zita had given him. He picked it up and began to read the diary of Margaret Ravenswood.

The journal started when she was seventeen and her father wanted her married to a forty-two-year-old curate with, as she put it, 'bristling brows, bad breath and a voice to turn an Archbishop pagan.' A few weeks away from marrying, she met Rohenga, one of the Samdhya, and fell powerfully in love with him.

Rohenga told her about his people: the Wildmark, they called themselves, but also the Storm and sometimes the Deep. Their true name, in their own tongue, was the Samdhya: the Holding Together.

He read her words avidly, finding in Margaret something of his own longing for change, and his own sense of being lost. He read so long his stomach rumbled, and he crept downstairs to sneak some hard bread rolls and butter.

Over the next few days, Tom fell into a routine. In the mornings, after breakfast, he dipped in and out of the diary. At eleven, he walked the boundaries with Kit, making the wards, the power of it becoming more and more a part of him, and he began to enjoy being with the quiet, strange, silver-haired boy whose pained, silver eyes held such depths.

The boundary walls were strong, and he poured more and more of himself into them, feeling Jack's dark wildness flashing around him.

Sometimes they would lie with flasks of fresh fruit juice that Kit made, under the spreading branches of the great oak tree, side by side, almost touching, and Kit would sing. He had a low, unearthly voice, with sad, lilting songs of a sort that Tom had never heard before.

'Where did you learn those?' Tom asked him one day.

Kit smiled. 'Mother did sing to me.'

For a while, everything was still and quiet. The summer solstice had long passed, but though the days were shortening, the evenings were long and clear, and Jack had his meals in his rooms, which Kit or Zita brought to him on a tray and cleared away for him, when he ate at all. Tom lived for the evenings, when he and Kit and Zita would sit by the side of the moat, dangling their legs down over the bank, sharing a roast chicken or some sausages. He did not see Jack; did not seek him out in his rooms.

Most days, Zita wafted through the house, putting records onto the gramophone, reading out from her collection of plays and making things from herbs and mosses and other plants. These, Tom realised now, were draughts to restore their energy after they had worked, as well as other kinds whose purpose he did not dare to guess at. Tom noticed that it was Zita who dealt with paperwork, letters and bills. It surprised him to see her one morning laboriously making out a cheque for the electricity company. Everything was in Zita's name; she had control of the accounts. Jack did sometimes get post, in a handwritten envelope, from a solicitor in the local market town, and Tom filed away this information, thinking that he should write to the firm or maybe even try to visit it.

Tom realised he hadn't looked at his mobile phone in days; it had run out of battery, and when he managed to charge it, there was still no reception.

A letter arrived from Fletcher, asking him if he needed anything, which Tom answered briefly but politely. He simply wrote that he was all right, and that if he did need anything, he'd be in touch. Somehow, the things he was encountering were too big and difficult to put into banal words on the page.

Kit offered to post it for him, as he took the horse and cart to the village shop every week, and Zita would occasionally accompany him to deal with things. As she put it one morning, 'Lolly, darling. Moolah.' Zita, it seemed, was allowed to go as far as the market town when necessary, about twice or three times a year.

Tom had a hankering to leave the grounds, and also he wanted to see if he would be permitted to do so. He thought of Zita's warning. He hadn't seen Jack for many days now, and the oppressive feeling had left him, although he still dreamed of music and light, and of strange, ever-decreasing spaces which led down into nothingness.

So one bright morning, when Leana was basking in the sunshine on the lawn, Zita was playing Mozart on the gramophone and Jack was brooding in the depths of his rooms, Tom clambered into the cart with Kit.

As the horse plodded down the drive, Tom watched the mound for any sign of movement. But there was nothing apart from the breeze in the trees.

The village was not far, and Tom, sitting beside Kit, enjoyed the air on his face.

As soon as they passed through the wards, Tom felt a change, and something happened to Kit: his speech became slower. There was a glamour on him, preventing him from speaking to anyone outside. Tom's heart filled with pity.

A single track with a line of grass down the middle led the way to the village, and they met nobody on the way, though they did pass the church, which had a lonely sign on it advertising Mass and a coffee morning.

Not for the first time Tom wondered if people kept away from Mundham Farm, sensing the wards somewhere at the back of their mind, like a high-pitched buzzing just out of hearing. There was probably a powerful glamour on it, he thought, deflecting unwelcome attention.

The village was really just a cluster of houses set away from the high street. There was a small supermarket, a couple of cars parked in front of it, another church and a bus stop. After tying up the old black horse to a post, they entered the supermarket.

Air-conditioning hit Tom, and he felt momentarily discomfited. There were a few people rustling through the aisles, and he was surprised that nobody gave Kit a second glance. They made their purchases, household items mostly, whose packaging reminded Tom with a pang of his normal life; a large sack of potatoes, rice and cooking oil. Everything smelled faintly of disinfectant.

When they'd finished, Kit produced a roll of twenty-pound notes and counted them out carefully.

'You up at the farm, then?' said the woman at the checkout to Tom. She was middle-aged, wearing a pinny, and had a streak of red-dyed hair. She looked jolly and her name, Tom noted from a badge on her lapel, was Sally. It struck him that this was the first time he'd spoken to anyone who wasn't Kit, Zita or Jack for a while.

'Yes. For the summer.'

'Ah, you must be the poor boy whose parents died. Oh, I am sorry.' She clucked.

Kit waved at him from outside. Tom managed to smile at the lady, who made no attempt to conceal her interest, staring at him with an arch expression as she counted through the notes, and he lugged the sack of potatoes out to the cart, where Kit was already loading up.

The horse blew out a deep breath as they finished, and a single decker bus in a dark green livery, looking old and weary, chugged up to the bus stop. It was full, mostly of people going shopping in the market town. Kit flinched, as if he could not stand the sound of the engine, and turned away.

An elderly lady with two sticks took her time getting off the bus, followed by a woman who seemed to have three or four children in various states of undress and with varying degrees of lollipops in their mouths, a small terrier-like dog yapping at her heels. The mother dropped her wallet, and someone hurried out from the bus behind her, thrusting a soft toy at her which had been left behind.

An idea came to Tom. Kit was busying himself with the packages. He dropped the bridle and sauntered over to the bus stop. And then, casually, he stepped up onto the bus.

'Ticket?' said the driver.

'To the town, please.' Tom felt in his pockets for change. His hands closed on a two-pound coin.

Almost immediately a terrible pain hit Tom in his stomach, and he doubled over. His vision went black. He grabbed on to the bus pole.

'You all right, son?' The driver, though concerned, was looking at his watch. Everyone else on the bus was either staring out of the window or tapping their feet. Somebody rustled through their shopping. A child asked, 'Why are we waiting, Mummy?' and then kept repeating 'Mummy'.

Kit came over. He grabbed Tom by the shoulders, helped him off the bus and sat him down gently on a bench by the stop.

'Is he getting on or not?' The bus driver sucked in his teeth.

'Not,' said Kit thickly.

The driver wrenched the bus into gear.

As soon as it had puttered round the bend of the road, Tom's pain vanished. He managed to stand up.

Tom didn't need to say anything to Kit. He knew what had happened. That was James, pulling him back, stopping him from going any further. He'd felt the wildness, the darkness.

James Swinton, his own flesh and blood.

The realisation hit him: he was trapped. He was a captive too, in the farm on the island.

Now he understood the sign on Zita's blazer, the square within the square. And within that square, another square, and so on, and on until there was nothing.

They were all trapped – he, Kit, Zita and the Captive – in Jack's web of power, and he was the spider at the centre, feeling the tension on the strings.

The woman in the shop was looking out at them, through the glass, her face distorted, and Tom thought she might be saying something; but he couldn't know, would never know.

Kit helped him gently up into the cart. He lay on his back and looked up at the sky as the horse slowly began to move off.

The future was forming inside him. An intention, bright and clear. No longer was there shadow and darkness. Now there was a point of light, and that light meant there was only one thing to do. Tom would find the Captive and release her.

Or else he would be a prisoner in Mundham Farm with Jack as his master for the rest of his life.

Chapter 10

2nd June, 1846

Wandering in the woods, I wished every tree were he. I picked up stones and kissed them, imagining that he had once held them. Perhaps he had. I feel his imprint everywhere. Sometimes I think he is watching me. Why, why does he stay away from me?

—From the diary of Margaret Ravenswood

As they drove slowly back to Mundham Farm, the gentle movement of the cart lulling him, Tom watched the still sky above him and resolved that he would wait until he was sure everyone was asleep, and then begin his search for the Captive that very night. He sat up and joined Kit on the driver's seat, saying nothing of his plan. Kit merely offered him wordless comfort, patting him on the shoulder, awkwardly, as if the gesture did not come naturally to him.

Tom hadn't, though, prepared for what Jack might do. When they returned to the farmhouse, the old man was standing in front of the main door, dressed in britches and a long black cloak, with a sword at his belt. Zita was behind him, looking downcast, clutching her shawl around her shoulders, her eyes dark with shadow.

Tom slid down from the cart and began to help Kit to unload things. He was about to enter the farmhouse when Jack blocked his way.

'You. My flesh and blood. You will be with me today.'

Tom dropped the heavy can of cooking oil he was carrying. 'I need to help Kit.'

'Kit can manage. He managed before without you. The whelp can manage again.'

Zita rushed forwards and hefted up the can, taking it in before Jack could say anything. Kit sent her a look of wordless thanks.

Jack's haggard face was stern, his eyes gleaming, his hand strong on Tom's shoulders. They went together into the gloom of the farmhouse hall, and Jack led him upstairs.

The smell in Jack's rooms was as musty and rich as ever. A mortar lay on a table, with some sweet-smelling herb half crushed inside it. An astrolabe was placed down to one side, as if Jack had just finished with it. There were many other things that, in other circumstances, Tom would have enjoyed looking at. The glass structure caught him off guard once more, and he stared at it, seeing both himself and Jack reflected in its surface. The way that Tom was standing his body seemed to cover Jack's entirely, and it was as if their faces merged together. Startled, Tom moved away.

Jack heaved a sigh. 'I will show you. What we have. What I, James Swinton, have. What you will have when I choose to go.'

'Why don't you free the Captive?' Tom spoke through his teeth.

The question made Jack turn and gaze at him, as if it had never occurred to him before. He spoke slowly, as if to a child. 'The moment I free her, she will kill me and you, and there will be a storm such as has never been seen.' He paced to the window. It was bright outside. 'Do you think they are like us? Do you think that because they look human that they are human?' He chewed his lips reflectively. 'They do not exist like us, think like us, eat like us. Their minds span centuries. We are nothing to them. They would squash us as we would a fly. *Umbra sumus*, Thomas. We are shadow. They are not. I thought they were of the divine essence. In past times I thought I was talking to angels. But they are not angels. They are something else.'

'What are they?'

Jack smirked. 'I do not know, but I worked long and hard to understand them.'

'Why don't they attack?'

'They cannot touch me. What I have done is unprecedented.' He studied Tom for a second. 'I have kept one of them and I have partaken in their essence. They tell me – Zita, Kit – that it has been four hundred years. To me – I have flown further and seen more. Sometimes it seems like a thousand years. Sometimes like the passing of a cloud in front of the sun. What am I but a mayfly on the surface of the stream? What am I but a pebble dropped into an ocean? Come.' He took Tom's wrist and held his hand gently, pulling him downwards to sit with him on a low brocaded sofa.

Jack bent forwards over a crucible, throwing in some powders he collected from jars, muttering all the while under his breath in a language that didn't sound English. He stood, lifted the ring of keys from his belt, selected a small one, opened a drawer in his desk. Tom shifted uncomfortably, interested all the same. The tick of the clock on the mantelpiece seemed slower than usual, the space between each beat expanding. With great care, Jack placed something onto the table between them.

It was a small jewelled wooden box. It seemed to fold space around itself, to be more fully here than the other things in the room. It made Jack appear younger, stronger. Tom felt dizzy looking at it.

When Jack placed two fingers on the box's lid, he sighed with pleasure, as if he had just taken a long refreshing drink.

'Now. You touch my hand. Don't touch the box.'

Tom did so and felt something like a low electric shock.

'Keep hold.'

There was a lurch, which Tom felt as a wrench in the deepest part of his being. There was a sensation of falling and something like a great wind.

When it passed, he looked around, expecting he did not know what.

They were in Jack's rooms. Everything was different. The light coming in through the windows was cleaner. There was no litter of objects, no sinister glass structure hanging from the ceiling. The furniture had all gone, the books, the desk. Instead there were two or three wooden presses set against the walls, and the tapestries hanging down were new and bright, and rushes covered the floor.

When Jack looked up Tom could not suppress a gasp. He was young. He looked very much like Tom.

It was as if he were looking in a mirror that was slightly askew. Tom shuddered.

There was now a lightness about Jack's movements, and he leapt upwards, smiling, and paced to the window and looked out, beckoning to Tom to follow.

Down below, in front of the house, with a bundle of wood in his arms, dressed in a loose white tunic and britches, with leather boots on, was a boy, his black hair closely cut.

'He cannot see us,' said Jack. 'I am here, somewhere. My younger self.'

'Who is it?' Tom peered down. 'That's not you, is it?' He felt a little dazzled by the implications.

The boy below, as if sensing something, glanced up at the window, and for a moment Tom was pierced with shock.

It was Kit. Kit as he had been before his hair grew long and silver.

The boy had not seen them; he was looking at a swallow swooping in front of the window; he shouldered his burden and went onwards.

They went downstairs. The layout of the house was different. Maidservants were sweeping the stone floor of the hall, one very young, with flaxen hair flat against her cheeks and an inquisitive look in her eyes; another much older, dark-haired, who was perhaps her mother, more watchful and slow. The same painting of William Swinton hung above the fireplace, but with no plaque. A black-and-white spaniel scampered through the hall, stopping right by them as if it could smell them, whimpered and moved on. Tapestries shifted gently, stirred by a breeze from the open door.

Jack and Tom stepped outside into the fresh sunlight.

Kit was making a stockpile of wood in a small shed that leant against the house. There was a smell of sewage, which made Tom's nose wrinkle. Beyond was a rumble of jerrybuilt buildings from which issued smoke and the pleasanter scents of cooking. Kit whistled as he worked and looked healthy and smiling. The spaniel came sniffing at his heels, and the boy stopped to ruffle its head. 'Here, lass.' The dog licked Kit's hand, evidently enjoying his company.

Then Tom experienced another deep rush of confusion, as coming round the corner of the house, dressed almost identically to the man who was standing next to Tom, was Jack.

Kit stiffened, slowed and then resumed his work.

'Kit,' said Jack's double.

'Master?' Kit stopped. He was sweating with the heat and he balanced his bundle of wood down on top of the pile. The spaniel, snuffling about, was kicked away by Jack.

'My preparations continue.'

'Master.'

'I have need of thee, boy.'

Kit was trembling and he swallowed, as if he were trying not to say something.

'Tha'rt afeared, boy.' Jack's double laughed, and Tom was horrified to see that Jack was laughing too. 'Tell thy master what affrights thee.'

Kit looked up and began piling the wood once more. 'They do, Master. Them in the woods. The … Good Folk.' He made a sign, as if averting their gaze from him.

'These be not the tales of children. This be not what thy mother tells thee as thou huddlst by her in the dark. This be the truth, and we shall be the first to find it. We begin on the morrow.'

'Nay,' said Kit quietly.

'I know what thou canst do, Kit. And I have need of thee.'

Jack's double grasped Kit by the shoulder and Tom saw terror in Kit's eyes.

Then there was another lurch, which Tom felt once more in his very guts, and they were back in Jack's rooms in the present day, and in Jack's bearing was triumph. The light in the room had not changed since they had left it; if they had even left it. Tom glanced quickly at the clock on the mantelpiece. Its hands had not moved since they'd gone.

Jack spoke slowly. 'That is all for today. I will show you more tomorrow.' He dismissed Tom with a brusque wave of his hand.

Tom wanted more. The need for it coursed through him. He saw the look of sly delight in Jack's expression. He could see anything, go anywhere. The whole of history was in his grasp.

'Thank you,' said Tom, not really knowing what else to say. The words seemed inadequate.

'Go now.' Jack turned his attention to some papers and began leafing through them.

Dismissed, and feeling as if he had done something wrong, Tom left the room and went to find Kit. He grasped the banister more tightly than usual and stared in wonder at the hall, its once familiar objects now rendered strange, as if a veil had been placed over them. He wondered if he could ever look at things in the same way again. Even the sun outside seemed older, more weary. He understood what Jack wanted. The hunger to know, to see. It filled him with awe. And also, somewhere, terror. He found himself glancing behind, in case Jack had followed him down. But he hadn't.

Kit was in the kitchen, scrubbing the table.

'He showed you, didn' he?'

'He did, Kit. He did. He showed me the house, as it was when it was built, I think. And he showed me something else. He showed me you.'

Carefully, as if he were afraid he might do harm with it, Kit placed the knife down and looked away from Tom.

'What happened?' Tom grabbed Kit by the shoulders, staring at him deep in his silver eyes. 'What did he do to you?'

Kit shook his head and pointed at his mouth.

'You can't say. You can't say because he's put some glamour on you.'

'We maun do the wards.'

'It's impossible!' Tom released him and put his hands over his face for a minute or two, breathing deeply. When he looked again, Kit was getting ready to go out.

So they set off to do the wards, the summer sun beating down mercilessly. Jack, presumably, was holed up in his rooms, moving through time and space.

The clocks in Mundham Farm chimed throughout the night. Zita had been quiet during their supper of tinned soup, tinned tuna, bread and boiled potatoes with the skin still on, and Kit had done all the clearing away whilst Leana dozed on her bed by the oil-fired range.

Tom had slipped up to his room as soon as he could. It was a warm night, and he opened both his windows and sat on his bed leafing through Margaret Ravenswood's diary, keeping an ear out for the chimes of the grandfather clock. He did not drift off, reading by the light of three flickering candles, his curtains gently flapping. Leana had come up with him and sat curled by his side, her ears twitching occasionally. She never offered her belly to be rubbed, but instead sat just near enough to him to be tickled if she wanted to be.

In the diary, Margaret described her meetings with Rohenga. The rector's daughter found him fascinating. He told her more and more about the Samdhya and what they did. They hunted something they called the Knot, but the entries were not very clear about what that might be; it only appeared every so often, but when it did, the Samdhya would muster and ride to find it. Most other times they seemed to feast and hunt the game in the woods.

One day, the diary simply stopped, three days before she was due to marry the awful curate. Tom closed the diary and found himself wondering what happened to her.

Had she run away with the Samdhya? Could a human join them?

Moonlight stole softly through the casement into his bedroom, and he could see almost as well as if by day. The house creaked and rustled, but he could hear no movement that might suggest people. They had all gone to sleep, he surmised; that is, if Jack ever slept.

After his parents drowned, he had stood outside their house, wishing and wishing that time would fall away and that he would be able to walk through the door and they would be there. There would his father be, sitting in the battered armchair by the television, looking busily through some papers for his court case the next day. Tom would come in, and his father would look up and smile. 'An easy win, this one,' he would say. And his mother would be in her study, finishing writing one of her lectures, and she would come down and they would have dinner together. It wouldn't be special, or different; it would just be normal. Cauliflower cheese, roast chicken, frozen peas. Things he had not eaten, the way his father cooked them, for years. He remembered the hum of the dishwasher, the soft orange light on the landing as he went to his bedroom.

A thought came to him. He could ask Jack. He could ask Jack if he could go back. Just once, to see them. He would not be able to touch them, talk to them, but he could see them before they drowned.

At the same time, clashing, contrasting, another thought surfaced. If he did that, then he would be beholden to Jack. Jack would have something over him. He would be able to let Tom see them, and Tom knew that once he had done so, he would not be able to stop.

For the first time in years, he sobbed, heavy, wracking sobs, and Leana came to him and snuffled her nose into his face, and he lay still, whilst she formed into a tight ball next to his head.

It was no good being like this, he thought, after a while. There was a way forward for him now. A way to break the chains that held everybody together.

It was now past midnight. Everyone was asleep. After a moment or two, he resolved that he would start his search in the cellar. And so he crept downwards. The house was in darkness and he went carefully, so as not to stumble. No music came from Zita's rooms. Tom realised that he did not know where Kit slept, and the thought held him back for a moment, as the silver-haired boy might be anywhere in the house. But then he continued down the stairs.

The door to the cellar was in the space under the stairs. Tom had a torch in his pocket, and as soon as he stood at the top of the steps going down, he switched it on. There was a dank smell and a dripping sound. The stairs were wooden and rickety, so Tom went gently. The beam from his torch was powerful, and he raked it over a brick floor and puddles.

A huddled shape in the corner made him jump but it was only a tarpaulin.

Apart from necessary household supplies, the cellar seemed to be empty. His foot splashed in a puddle, and Tom cursed under his breath. Nobody, nothing, was down here.

He stood for a minute, feeling the cold, imagining the moat flowing around him in the darkness. It really was just a cellar. It was clear nobody came down here, except when they went to bring up tins of tuna, tomato soup and bottles of wine for Jack when they were needed. Tom shivered, sniffed in the mushroomy tang and clambered back up the stairs. He was glad to leave it and closed the door gently behind him.

Standing in the dim hallway, he could make out the shape of the grandfather clock and of the painting above the fireplace of William Swinton. Now, he thought, he could hear music. Was it the notes of a pipe playing? Or could it be Zita, awake, sitting at her windowsill? The sound made his skin shiver, wild and soft at the same time. He remembered the carved wooden flute in his room. He crept back up the stairs, trying as far as possible not to make them creak, and stood uncertainly on the first-floor landing.

All old houses seem to breathe and move, and Mundham Farm was no different. He trod on a board which gave a loud whine. As still as he could manage, he hung back in the recesses of the landing; but he heard no footsteps. He breathed out.

Tom edged along the corridor. There were several doors on this landing and coming off it were smaller corridors, including to his own room, and one leading to Jack's rooms. The stairs up to the attic went from by Zita's room. The pipe music was still faint, and he wondered if it was even coming from inside the farmhouse at all. No lights shone from any of the doors, so Tom pressed on across the landing.

The stairway to the attic looked impossibly dark. But he had faced the cellar; whatever was up in the attic could surely be no worse.

He put his foot onto the first step, and then the second, telling himself all the time that he was being ridiculous, that nobody would wake up, and at the same time that there couldn't possibly be anybody up in the attic, as he would have heard or seen something. He turned the corner, his eyes now adjusted to the dark, and came up onto the attic floor.

The music was nearer now, surely. There were four or five doors here. Tom steeled himself. His torch made small pools of light. He counted the doors. Hang on – were there six? He must be going crazy. He turned to his left and shone the beam onto the wall, moving it slowly to the right. As he drew it across the walls, his hand began to shake. There were seven doors. His mouth was getting dry. The note of the flute was wilder now, impossibly yearning. Where were the stairs? They seemed further away.

The shadows on the walls grew larger, stretching into forms that seemed to warn. Putting his hand out behind him, panicking, he managed to locate the banister rail, and, holding onto it as if it were a lifebelt, he inched his way back down.

As soon as his feet touched the first-floor landing, his mind cleared. The moon was shining through the mullioned window, and he sat down carefully on the wooden settle. The ticking of clocks echoed throughout the entire house.

Tom switched his torch off and sat in the darkness. He'd had some kind of mental attack, clearly. How could the attic grow larger? It was impossible. But there could be magic at play. He sighed. It was late – too late. He'd tried to do too much on one night only.

He was imagining things. There was no music – how could there be anyone here playing the flute? How could the Captive be in the attic, in any case? He would have heard something in the day time. When he'd been in the house, in his bedroom, he'd heard nothing above him apart from the groans that the ancient beams made and the rushing and sighing of the wind through the chimneys.

Slowly, and very carefully, he made his way back to his room, and was obscurely relieved to find that it was exactly as he had left it. Leana was still curled up by his pillow. The cover on his bed was turned down, the imprint of his body exactly as he had lain. He threw himself onto the mattress.

He would try upstairs again when the sun was out.

Before he undressed, he looked out of the window, out across the moat, in which the moon's shimmering reflection hung, and found himself uttering the words of a prayer, which he had not done since he was a little boy at school.

'And deliver us from evil. For thine is the kingdom, the power and the glory, for ever and ever. Amen.'

When he'd finished, his mind jumping to the last time he'd seen his parents, he went to where he had hidden the flute, taking it out of the drawer. To his surprise, it was warm, as if it had just been played. He slipped it back in the drawer, under the photos and letters.

He slept with his bedside lamp turned on, the golden wash of light making a pool on the scuffed wood of the bedside table. He was gladder than ever for Leana.

Chapter 11

8th June, 1846

The day of the wedding draws nearer. The cake has been ordered. Cousin Millicent is to be bridesmaid. Her giggles are grating. I have not yet tried on my dress. It hangs in the wardrobe, limp and white. I stare out of my window whilst mother fusses with my clothes. I believe Rohenga has forgotten me.

—From the diary of Margaret Ravenswood

The next morning, when Tom came into the kitchen at just past eight, he saw that Kit was out already, tending to the horse in the field beyond the moat.

Zita, the silver bracelet still on her wrist, was stirring a bowl of porridge slowly, muttering something to herself. There was a sick, tight feeling in Tom's stomach. He listened carefully to the sounds of the house, dreading Jack's heavy step down the stairs.

And yet at the same time he longed to be transported back, to feel the weight of modernity fall away, to the house as it had been in the year it had been built.

He yawned.

'The air was so much lighter then,' he said, taking a bowl from Zita's hands. She sat down opposite him, looking at him with that slightly sideways appraisal. 'The light… It was like you could tell the sun was younger. I could almost feel the world turning.'

'He showed me too,' said Zita, 'when I first came here.'

'And how did you get here? How long have you been here? Five hundred years, like Jack and Kit?'

Zita lapped at her porridge delicately, pausing to pour milk onto it, making a puddle. 'I used to do this in the nursery,' she said. 'Nanny always hated me doing it and used to threaten me with the hairbrush. She was a dear old thing, though, and never really spanked me.'

'You're the best at not answering questions.' Leana came to him and put her head on his knee. He scratched her head, and she closed her eyes with pleasure.

Sighing theatrically, Zita drew her shawl over her face. 'I am Al-Shabar, concubine to the Sultan.'

'Now you're just being silly.'

'I like to keep you on your toes. Well, now, let me see. How long have I been here?' She cleared her throat, and her eyes were suddenly full of sorrow. 'When I was born, the good old widowed queen was still just on the throne.'

'Victoria? Queen Victoria?' Tom could not keep the note of surprise out of his voice, even despite what he had seen so far. How many years ago was that? Over a hundred. He put his spoon down.

Zita removed a locket from around her neck, and placed it on the kitchen table, turning it over so that Tom could see the inscription on the back.

'ZAR, 1900,' Tom read out. Once more his head began to spin, and he clutched the kitchen table for support.

'You want to hear my story?' she murmured, stroking the locket gently. Tom nodded. She gathered herself together. 'Then I'd better make some more tea.'

She went about the tea as if it were a ceremony, boiling the kettle till it whistled, pouring the water over tea-leaves in a pot, and setting out tea-cups and a bowl of sugar with silver tongs, beside a little silver milk jug in the shape of a cow. 'Now we must wait until it brews. Nanny would be awfully cross if I didn't let it brew properly.'

They sat in silence for a few minutes, Zita contemplating her hands, and Tom staring into his distorted reflection on the sugar bowl. Eventually, Zita roused herself. 'I'll be mother,' she said, an ironic gleam in her eye, and poured out a dark golden stream of tea into her cup first, and then into Tom's.

'Tell me what happened.' Tom leaned forwards. 'I have to know.'

She sighed, taking a sip, the cup held lightly in her slender fingers. 'He was looking for someone like me. Things happened around me, you see, that couldn't be explained.'

'What kind of things?'

Zita glanced at Tom with her dark eyes, and once more he felt a frisson of something electric ripple through his entire body.

'Promise not to hate me, darling?' She pouted.

'I promise.' *How could I?* thought Tom. *How could I hate you?*

'There was a man in the village who kept budgerigars – about twenty of them, in a cage. He would let you in to see them, and Nanny and I would often go and feed them. They were rather sweet little things, all flying up and down, and then they'd sit on their perches with their heads on one side, as if studying you. But I couldn't stand it. I couldn't stand to see them in that cage.' Leana stretched her limbs on her bed, and Zita absently reached out to stroke her.

'One night, before I went to bed, I knelt down by my bedside. At first I was just praying – we'd always been taught to pray, you know. God bless Mummy, God bless Daddy, God bless Archie at school and God bless Nanny… and there, normally, I would stop. I kept going, thinking about the birds. And the prayer started to become something else.

'Suddenly I wasn't in the nursery, and Nanny wasn't sitting behind me in her armchair. I was in the man's house in the village, and I could really see the cage. It was dark – and of course when I'd been there earlier it hadn't been dark at all.

'And all the birds saw me, and none of them made the slightest sound, as if they'd almost been expecting me. So naturally I lifted the latch, and they still all sat there, and then I realised I'd have to open the window as well.'

She paused and fiddled with her teaspoon.

'And when I did, out they all flew, in a perfect little stream. Then I pictured my bed, and there I was again. Of course I thought it had been a dream. But the next morning, when I woke up, I felt sick. Really sick, with a terrible pain in my stomach and a feverish mind. I could hardly move, either. As I lay there, with a black-coated doctor fussing over me, his big leather bag open on the bed, and Nanny flapping around getting in the way, a little budgerigar hopped onto my windowsill. It looked at me sideways and then flew away. And I knew. I knew I'd done it.'

'That was the first time you did it. And Jack found you that way?'

'He sensed it happen. He can feel things like that. He watched me for, oh, years. I must have been seven when it first happened. I thought it was a silly game. I called it "sending". I didn't really know the power of it. I was very careful not to cause confusion – but it always made me ill. When I was at school, once or twice I played tricks on the mistresses – putting things in locked rooms, things like that. But honestly, my darling, the pain of it was too much to bear.' She placed the tea-cup down and began fiddling with the sugar tongs. 'I didn't do it for years. Then my twenty-first birthday party arrived. My cousin Bunny Vere was staying, with a party down from the Varsity. They were all mostly boating yahoos, who roared and played billiards and smoked and cheeked me.

'But not John Temple. He was different from the others. He was slender, dark-haired. He'd come up from a grammar school in Kent. The others would rag him about it dreadfully, but he didn't mind. He just carried on doing what he did best. He had a look, a kind of burning, innocent look.

He was reading a poem –"Gerontion" it was called. By a chap called Eliot. Rather a new thing, back then. How well I remember those words.' She put her shawl over her head, and for a moment, the old, lively Zita was back as she declaimed some lines from the poem.

Then she took the shawl off and placed it back over her bare shoulders. 'John didn't say anything to me that morning at breakfast, but he dropped his toast, and marmalade went all over his dear white trousers, and he looked so sweet and confused when he picked it up … Anyway, I'm babbling, forgive me.' Tears were trembling in the corners of her eyes. 'There was a feeling in my heart, like wings. All I could think about was John and how I would dance with him. There was something special in him, like a flame. I knew my mother didn't approve of him – she wanted someone with money or a title, or preferably both, not some son of a Kentish greengrocer.

'That night, I sent myself to him as he lay in his bed. I don't really know why. He wasn't frightened. He stretched out his hand, and I stretched out mine, and then I left him. Of course next morning at breakfast he thought it was just a dream. The way he looked at me, I knew that he loved me. And what was strange was that it hadn't made me tired – I wasn't tired at all.

'I went for a walk, just after I got dressed. I liked to be alone before parties. I walked for ages, through the village, over the fields, feeling as if I were skirting something huge, something vast and important. It was the most glorious day,

Tom, the sun beaming down. And I heard music – the most wonderful music, Tom, you would not believe it.'

Tom stiffened a little, but did not mention the flute he had heard or the one he had been given.

Zita continued. 'I'd heard rumours about Mundham Farm – an old man lived there, an eccentric who saw nobody, they said, with a beautiful silver-haired servant who hardly ever spoke. I came past Uriah Fiske's pigs, and paused to scratch one of them with a long stick, then through Long Pightle, which Captain Urquhart had let go fallow, and by the Home Field of Mundham Farm, and saw the house.

'It was about six o'clock in the evening, and there were lights blazing in every window, though the sun was still out. I don't know what I was thinking – that I would ask the music player to come to my party. Something in that music, Tom, entered my soul and pulled me onwards. I walked through the field as if in a dream, and as I walked, I realised that all thoughts of home were leaving my mind, and only the farm and the music were what I wanted.

'I stood at the edge of the bridge.'

At this point, she bent her head and when she looked up again, tears were flowing down her cheeks. Tom laid a hand on her arm, and she took his with her own, entwining their fingers.

'Behind me was my twenty-first birthday and Bunny Vere and John Temple and T.S. Eliot and cocktails and dances and my silly schoolfriends Moggy and Janey and my mother's social climbing and my father's county duties.

But those things all seemed to melt away in the music, to become shadows, empty. As I set foot on the bridge, I felt something pass through me – a shock or a wave of power.

'The back door was open. I came into the hall, and Kit was there, sweeping the stone floor. He looked up, and I had never seen such sadness in a man's eyes before. Those silver eyes… He didn't say anything. And I think, for a minute or two, a teeny, tiny minute, I fell in love with him.'

She sipped slowly from her cup.

'And that was that. At first I rather enjoyed it, you know. Jack showed me all the things he has shown you, and more.' There was an intensity, a longing, in her gaze that troubled Tom for a moment; and then it passed. 'I started learning about the plants and things in the woods. I didn't know about the Captive, of course, and Kit couldn't tell. I started to be able to make draughts, and to send myself to places with a quicker recovery. It felt like one long day, sometimes, and then at other times like months. One morning, I remember, after Jack had taken me to the shores of Troy, I suddenly had an image in my mind, of my mother. And then I remembered her, and how worried she would be. I tried to leave.'

'Your parents? John Temple? Did they not come looking for you?'

'Jack put a glamour on me. I didn't know until a policeman came up the drive. I saw him get off his bicycle. I'm not sure I realised how much time had passed, because Jack had been showing me things. He was quite handsome, as policemen go, and I remember thinking he looked more like a matinee idol than a sergeant. He pushed his bicycle across the bridge and left it leaning against the post. He banged on the door, and as nobody answered immediately, I went down. I stood right in front of him, and said, 'What can I do for you?' I knew he was looking for me. But he couldn't see me. He called up the stairs, and eventually Jack appeared, ignoring me, and told the policeman he hadn't seen anything.

'I was furious after that, darling. And it was worse when a day or two later I was walking in the fields, trying to find a way out, and I saw John Temple coming along. He looked distracted. He was holding his book of poems – the one he'd read to me out of. And I called to him and shouted over the hedge, but I could not get near him. Once I thought he stopped, puzzled, as if he'd heard something in his innermost heart. And I knew then that he did really love me, because he had heard me, distant though I was.'

She took her silver locket off her neck and opened it. Inside was not a lock of hair, as Tom had been expecting, or a portrait, but a folded piece of paper. Zita flattened it out carefully and showed it to him.

It was an obituary from *The Times*, dated January 1982. It was yellowing and printed in close type. It had been very neatly clipped.

'Sir John Temple,' she read out. 'Look, isn't the picture sweet? Doesn't he look lovely? He was so splendid, like a young lion. But you can see it in his eyes – a look of longing. I sent myself to him for years. Sometimes dressed as a clerk, sometimes as a passerby, sometimes sitting in court, watching him. Of course I could never stay long, and I'm sure that he wondered about things. He would notice me, and then I would leave. Perhaps he thought he was dreaming.

'He became a barrister – one of the best of his genera-tion – and then a judge. He did marry of course – a horsey, county type, gum-boots and dogs. Five children. Lady Temple sounds well, does it not? Mummy would have been proud. I sent myself to his funeral – it was the only time I was able to sit there as myself, in the black dress that I had been wearing when he met me. When I came back, I could not move for three days.'

Tom held Zita's hand. She sobbed into his shoulder.

The grandfather clock in the hall struck the hour, and the obituary fluttered to the ground.

Chapter 12

1st June, 1846

Mother was vexed with me all day, as she found out I'd lost my pearl hatpin. I could not tell her where it had gone.

—From the diary of Margaret Ravenswood

Whenever Tom could, he would return to his room, and sitting down on his bed, pull out from his bedside drawer the dog-eared photograph of himself, his mother and his father.

In it, he was almost twelve years old. It had been taken about a week before the accident. Tom, holding both their hands, was smiling shyly somewhere to the side; his parents were both grinning. They were in France, getting ready for their expedition. He was wearing a white T-shirt and a baseball cap.

Tom had wanted so much to go with them. They would cross the Atlantic in a boat for two people. Tom had begged and pleaded with them to let him join in. They had been firm, though. Tom's father and mother were experienced sailors; a boat would be near by them all the time; they would be tracked and watched, their experiences filmed, their day-to-day lives broadcast across the world. It was for charity, as much as it was for their own sense of adventure.

Everything was predicted, everything planned out down to the last iota.

Everything, that is, except the weather.

They could not have predicted the sudden storm that came from nowhere and spun their boat as if it were a toy; the breakage of their radio; the capsizing of their boat and the inability of the rescuers to find them in the darkness.

He wanted to see them – to be near them again. To see them on the boat. To hold their hands once more. Would Jack be able to bring Tom to them?

Is that what Jack did, he wondered. Revisit the past endlessly, looking back at people he had once known. How it must all be blurred and strange now. Perhaps he could not even really tell the difference between the past and the present.

He felt trapped. One thing he realised was that he would not be able to find the Captive, release her and defeat Jack without help. And that would mean enlisting Zita or Kit – or both. He knew that they both hated Jack; but also that they were in thrall to him.

The memory of the girl in the woods came to him. He could also try to contact her again.

As he was eating toast and deliberating one morning in the kitchen after doing the wards with Kit, he was summoned once more to Jack's rooms.

He climbed up the stairs two by two. When he entered Jack's rooms, his uncle was sitting in his usual place behind his desk and, looking up, smiled at him. Tom was momentarily taken aback.

'Sit down.' Jack indicated the chair with a brisk nod. Without ceremony, he brought out the jewelled box again, and Tom sensed the slight shift in reality he had felt before, as if a weight were being placed down on a sheet, drawing everything towards it. Jack sighed, and placed his hand on it once more, and Tom, without needing to be told, touched the old man's hand with his own right hand.

A shudder of pain coursed through Tom's body.

'Hurts, don't it?' gasped Jack, wheezing deeply. Tom wondered if it got worse each time. How much did it hurt Jack then? How often had he done this, over the centuries? The old man's whole body was tense.

Then came the wrenching feeling, as if Tom was about to faint.

When it had faded, he felt the light on him again, the bright, clean light, and Tom knew they were in the past.

'Come.' Jack, youthful and vigorous, was striding out of the room.

The house, newly built, seemed much less confusing than its modern incarnation, and Tom started to wonder whether it had somehow extended itself over time, building up layers of internal rooms that were powered by the glamours that surrounded it, as if it were a living thing. Perhaps the Captive was in one of those rooms, hidden beyond sight, beyond the normal course of the senses. Tom despaired of ever being able to find her.

Perhaps Jack had poured his energy into the house, as he had put himself into the wards. The thought left him, as now, entranced by the sweet air and the pale light, he followed Jack outside.

This time there were no maidservants. The constant background hum of machinery and cars that could be heard even in the fields at Mundham was a dream. Tom's heart lifted. He saw that across the field a carpet of blue and white flowers was opening its petals to the sun. The blue flowers. He wondered what they meant.

'All the servants are gone,' said Jack. 'I sent them all away. All but for Kit.'

And suddenly there was Kit, with his black hair, and there was the younger version of Jack, standing by him, his hand on his shoulder. They had a sack, from which poked some iron bars and other things. The younger Jack sported a sword at his belt.

'Watch.' As he stood at Tom's side, Jack's breath was heavy. Tom kept expecting Kit and the younger Jack to notice them. It was strange: he could feel everything around him, but he knew that he was not imprinting the stones or the air with anything of himself. It was almost as if they were in a bubble: a capsule, floating through time.

'Master,' said Kit. Tom was surprised by how gentle and smooth his voice was. 'I shall not do it. I shall not take any of Them.' A wood pigeon cooed and fluttered its wings. The sound of someone chopping wood came from far off.

'Dost deny me, Christopher Last? Dost deny thy master?' Jack held Kit's face in his hand and gazed at him deep in the eyes.

For a moment Kit seemed to shrink. His shoulders sagged. He placed the sack down and its contents clanged. There was a smell of woodsmoke in the air.

He said simply, 'I cannot do it, Master.'

Jack released him and cursed once.

'Thou hast the gift, Christopher Last. Thou hast the gift and thou knowst I have need of thee.'

'I cannot do it.' Tom was amazed at Kit's firmness. Even when Jack drew his sword and held it at Kit's throat, Kit simply pushed it away, knelt and closed his eyes.

'End my life here, and I shall make my peace with my Lord. Forgive me, O God, for I have sinned.' He crossed himself.

That seemed to make Jack laugh, and he placed his sword carefully back into its scabbard. Kit opened his eyes. Tom saw his throat was shivering, and tears were flowing down his cheeks.

Jack made a gesture, muttered some words and drew a small circle in the air. A silver ring appeared, floating, between Jack and Kit.

'Devilry,' Kit sobbed. 'O Jesu, save me!' The silver ring floated towards him, solidifying as it did so, and then settled on Kit's wrist. He screamed in pain. 'Sorcerer! Servant of Beelzebub!'

'Shalt come along with me now. Thou dost not ken of what thou speakst.'

The older Jack, by Tom's side, had not moved or changed his expression.

Now his younger self strode forwards over the field towards the woods. Kit appeared to be dragged behind him. Tom knew where they were going.

Things around them began to shake and shiver, and then they were back in Jack's rooms. Tom wondered if it was getting harder and harder for Jack to go back, for the old man seemed briefly a frail shadow of himself, resting his head on the desk.

Once more Tom felt bereft. The sound of a plane in the sky above the house made him clutch his head. It was too loud, too strange. He began to see why Kit hated mobile phones so much; why he had shrunk from the bus, and the smell of oil. All the noise, all the bustle of the twenty-first century seemed so clangorous and empty.

After a minute or two he looked up, to see Jack, haggard and ancient, with a small smile on his face.

'Is there anything you wish? Anything in all of time.'

Tom nodded slowly and sat up.

'Show me.'

Tom took the photograph of his father and mother out of his pocket and placed it on the table.

Jack sighed. 'Your father. I had no need of him. He had no gift. Perhaps I should have tried to know him. You want to see them. Your mother.'

'You could have saved them? Could you save them?'

'I could have changed nothing. I can change nothing. But if you want to see them ...' Jack stood up, and paced towards the window, where once more he stood in the dappled light, looking out across the lawn towards the woods. 'There is a price.'

Tom shivered. He felt a great desire to touch the jewelled box. Jack would be able to show him his parents – and everything else. The whole universe opened up in front of him.

'What else can I see?'

Then Jack turned round with a terrible grin on his face. 'I can show you everything. I can show you the birth of our Saviour Lord Jesus Christ, when the world shook. I can show you his death, when the world wept. I can show you Good Queen Bess riding a white palfrey through the woods to meet her lover. I can show you the antique emperors, and Julius Caesar murdered in the Senate. I can show you the stones of Stonehenge raised up. I can show you all that is past, anywhere in the world.'

'Anywhere?'

Jack snorted. 'Anywhere – and beyond. The things the Samdhya know are things that no man has known, nor ever will ...' His eyes shone, and Tom saw in them a much younger man, a man full of a thirst for knowledge. 'There are spheres of light and power and radiance.' He paused. 'Angelic, crystalline, divine.'

The possibilities were dizzying. 'And ... the future?'

'What is to come?' He tapped his fingers on the windowsill. 'Glimpses, shadows. Nothing is carved into stone. Time is a river. What is past is frozen; what is to come, still rushes. *Panta rei.*'

Tom had done enough Greek to know what that meant. 'Everything flows.'

'I can show you everything. But if you want to see your parents, then ...' He turned and faced Tom fully. 'You must become my bondsman.'

'Like Kit?'

'Not like Kit. You will become my bondsman and my indentured apprentice, and I will show you everything, and you will continue the family line.'

'What do you mean?'

'You will continue the family line – you will set up home here, and a family.'

'But how am I to continue it?'

Jack sighed. 'I had thought that I might do so with Zita. But it must be true, and I will not force her.'

The world around Tom trembled. 'You'll show me my parents – if I agree to do what you want? If I agree to ... become you?'

Jack, shadows casting his face, folded his arms and laughed, once.

'Yes, my pretty boy. Yes, my pretty sweeting.'

'And if not?'

'You have seen, boy, what happens to people who disobey me.'

The bird in the cage, the spider in the web.

'Now. There is more. The manipulation of energy, the discovery of powers, the ability to see into and through the obsidian glass, into where the Samdhya go, and what they see ...' He drifted off once more, as if he were now somewhere entirely elsewhere. Tom stood, fixed, like the hare that Leana had almost caught. He coughed, and Jack noticed him once more and spoke abruptly. 'You had better eat your supper.'

Evening sunlight, slanting through the windows. Leana, coming to meet him at the bottom of the stairs. The kitchen door was open, and the welcoming scent of slowly cooking oniony stew met Tom's nostrils; Zita had put the gramophone on gently, playing a Mozart piano concerto, and Kit was at work chopping carrots.

Tom felt a sudden and overwhelming rush of love for both of them, and sank down into one of the ratty old kitchen chairs. Zita flicked a teatowel at him.

'What's the matter, old boy? You look like you've seen a ghost.'

Tom almost said that he had. Kit, Zita, Jack. What were they but ghosts, visitors from another time, remnants of centuries past? The jewelled box. Energy poured from it. Tom kept thinking about it, and coming back to it, all through supper, letting juice drip down his chin so that Zita scolded him and threw him a napkin.

Could it be possible that Jack had somehow trapped the Captive inside it? It was surrounded by iron bands.

Tom shuddered at the thought of it. The more he thought about it, the more likely it seemed.

He remembered his dream, of the light and the music.

They went to bed early that night, and for once Tom did not dream about the house; instead he dreamt of his parents. Little things: their voices, their clothes, their eyes, which he had thought he might have forgotten, or remembered wrongly, came to him. His mother, stroking his hair when he was ill with a fever. His father, reading a comic book to him.

But in the dream they would slip away, around a corner, and when he followed them, he would find an empty room.

Leana woke him up. She was moaning, in her strange, musical, lurchery way, and scrabbling at his door to get out. He could hear footsteps on the landing outside, and then Zita's voice. He stumbled out of bed and into the corridor, still in his boxer shorts and T-shirt.

The thumping noise that Kit had told him was bird scarers was pounding in from outside.

Zita was carrying a candle in a lantern; her face looked eerie in the glow. Kit had appeared from somewhere, fully dressed; but there was no sign of Jack. Leana slipped downstairs.

'They're not bird scarers, are they?' said Tom as they huddled on the top of the landing.

'Drums.' Zita bit her lip. 'War drums.'

They hurried to the window in the hall. The moon was behind a cloud. From across the island they could see dozens of points of flame from candles. All held in the hands of Samdhya.

'Are they attacking now?'

'The wards are strong. Tom 'n' I did them in the afternoon.'

They stood, uncertain, at the window whilst the beat of the drum jangled their nerves.

'Someone's standing at the end of the bridge,' said Tom. In the flickering candlelight, a tall, shadowy figure had separated from the mass of Samdhya, and was leaning on the gate.

'I think the darlings want to talk. Let me deal with them.' Zita strode to the door and began pulling open the bolts. Kit went to stop her, but she shoved him away.

'We'll all go,' said Tom, firmly, though his stomach was twisting and his mouth was dry. He pulled on boots, which rubbed against his bare shins, and put on a Barbour. Zita was wearing a silk kimono with a red dragon on the back, and red slippers. Her hair was tousled. Not for the first time, Tom wondered if Kit ever slept. The boy's silver eyes were gleaming with anticipation and his hair seemed to glow.

Outside it was cool, and a bright gibbous moon had appeared. The Samdhya, arrayed on the other side of the bridge, stilled their drumming and stood in ranks, flames flickering light across their faces.

They seemed to be countless, to stretch all the way across the field towards the woods. There were animals among them too. Was that a leopard, lifting its elegant head towards them? Was that a stag, head piled high with antlers? There was certainly a hare, strange aerial ears high and twitching, sitting quietly by the bank of the moat. Leana bristled and shrank back to a line of shrubs.

The three of them came slowly over the lawn towards the house end of the bridge. They were now separated from the mass of Samdhya only by a few feet of wood. And the water, thought Tom. Behind them the house was in darkness.

'They can't cross over the water, remember,' Zita whispered as they arrived.

The Samdhya at the other end, Tom realised with a gentle lurch of recognition, was the same one who had spoken to him on the path behind his school.

'The Swinton whelp,' he hissed. 'But forgive me.' His accent was strange, as if the words came to him with difficulty. 'My name is Rohenga.'

The name of the Samdhya who had met Margaret Ravenswood.

'The Hawk in the Mist,' sighed Zita.

'I have a message for you, Thomas Swinton. We have been hunting the Knot, and we are near to finding it. And when we do …' He held out his hand. In it, a ball of light was forming. 'This water will not stop us.'

The drums began to beat, wilder and wilder, and a wolf howled.

'In some ways we have already found it. In some ways we have already broken through your wards, and over the water, and into your house. In some ways we have already smashed open the prison and released our sister. Your kinsman James Swinton lies dead. And you three …'

A great shout arose from the Samdhya. The drumming and the howling intensified.

Rohenga pressed forwards. The wards around the gate shimmered and went silver as his face pushed right into them. Tom felt Rohenga's power in his own body, in his own essence.

'You three are his creatures. Thomas Swinton, you are James Swinton, as an acorn is an oak. We will come, and we will take you. Three times the sun will rise and set, and then the Knot will be found.'

Rohenga retreated and, taking aim, flung a ball of flame at the wards. The impact drained Tom, and he staggered, clutching at the bridge for support.

Throwing his head back, Rohenga opened his throat and let out a war cry that seemed to go on for ever, and the countless Samdhya joined in.

Zita's arm snaked around Tom's shoulders; and then, when he looked up, the whole expanse in front of him was empty.

Not a single Samdhya remained.

Chapter 13

9th June, 1846

I had a dream last night. He was with me – Rohenga. He said my name, and he talked of something called the Knot. What it is, I do not know. But it fills me with hope.

—From the diary of Margaret Ravenswood

Kit, Zita and Tom did not sleep that night, but sat in the kitchen, candles lit all along the windowsills, drinking cups of sweet tea that Zita seemed to be able to conjure from nowhere. Tom suspected that she was filling the pot with herbs for sustenance too, as he felt immeasurably better after the first cup. They did not feel tired, and waited for the dawn to come.

Kit and Tom, as soon as there was light, went out and strengthened the wards, and once more, Tom felt Jack's malign consciousness in the silvery weft and warp of the power.

'What did they mean, the Knot?' said Tom, when they had returned to the kitchen. He slumped into a chair. 'It sounds familiar.' Kit sat, mutely regarding his hands.

Leana was licking her belly on her bed by the range, seemingly unperturbed by the whole experience.

Zita looked puzzled. 'I'm not sure. Margaret Ravenswood mentions it somewhere.'

'The diary is in my room. I'll get it.'

A few minutes later, Tom had returned with the volume and they leafed through it. Once more, Tom found himself sympathising with Margaret's plight. Her portrait of Rohenga was so different from what they had seen of him.

'Why is he nice to her?' said Tom when they had found the passage.

'Who knows?' answered Zita. 'Their ways are mysterious. As she says – they see everything at once. Jack had held the Captive already for two hundred years or so by this point – maybe Rohenga thought Margaret could help him release her.'

'What do they say about the Knot?' asked Tom.

'Not very much. It's something they hunt from time to time.'

'Like an animal?' Tom bent over the pages, trying to see.

'No – it seems more like some kind of passage that allows them to bypass normal restrictions.'

'You mean – with it they can cross water?'

'Yes – and wards too.'

They would be able to come into the house. Tom shuddered. Perhaps that was what Jack knew, and that was why Jack was giving up – he knew his time was nearly up.

'So Jack wants to get out before they get in. And he wants me in his place! So I can be killed?'

He rose abruptly from the kitchen table and hurried blindly out through the hall and up the stairs to his room.

There he found Leana, sitting on his bed, and he buried his face in her flank.

It was some time before noon. He hadn't heard the clocks chime for a while. He turned over and stared at the ceiling. And as he stroked Leana, he remembered the hare she'd chased; and then the wooden flute with the hare carved into the end. It could help him. She could help him. He reached for it where he'd stashed it in a drawer.

Trembling, he placed it to his lips and blew.

At first the sound was breathy. Then, after a couple more tries, he made a low, pure note, and he placed his fingers over the holes. The holes had been spaced on a scale different from any that Tom knew. He played them from bottom to top, and the notes that came out rose and fell in a way that thrilled his spine pleasurably.

Leana started to growl, her whole body tensed, and her hackles rose.

Tom's stomach overturned, and the walls of the house seemed to fall away.

He was standing in a clearing in the woods near the farm. The leaves on the trees were browning, though it was summer. The sky above was bruise-grey and heavy.

Coming across the grass, nose twitching, was a hare. It paused. Tom watched it and was somehow not surprised when the hare vanished, and in its place stood the Samdhya girl. She was wearing a long, dark green tunic, and this time gold around her neck and wrists. She loomed, taller than Tom, and her dark eyes flashed at him. Tom remembered what Margaret Ravenswood had written about the eyes of the Samdhya, and he turned his head away.

'You left me the flute – it was a message.'

'They are near to finding the Knot now. It is a terrible thing.'

'Why so?'

She trembled. 'It will allow us to break down the wards, enter the house and release the Captive. But the price is high.' The wind rustled through the branches.

'What is it?'

She spoke quietly. 'One of the Samdhya is chosen to represent the rest. When the Knot arrives, if we go through, one of us must be cast out from the Samdhya.'

'Is that so bad?'

'To be torn from the wonders we know? To grow weak and to die? We do not die, Thomas Swinton. We can only be killed.'

'Is that what happened to the Captive? She was discarded by your tribe?'

She shook her head. 'No. Your master, James, stole her from us. James trapped her with powers we did not understand. She was in the form of a fox, and James came with Kit Last, and they wove wards and powers and took her and bound her.'

'You remember it?'

She looked at him oddly, as if that was a question she had never been asked.

'I have seen it.'

'So if the Samdhya find the Knot, and use it to break through to the farm, they will have to abandon one of you to mortality?'

'Yes,' she sighed. A buzzard mewed overhead. 'It will be me. I have been chosen.' She turned away from him.

'What if you do not go willingly?'

'I must go willingly.' She looked vulnerable for a moment, this proud warrior woman with her bow and arrow and her dagger at her belt. 'I would like you to help me.'

'You want me to find the Captive and release her?'

She nodded. 'I can give you help.'

'I don't want to be like him. Like Jack.' Though even as he said it, he thought of his parents and being able to see them whenever he liked. 'I've tried to find her. I can't. There doesn't seem to be room for her in the house.'

'That's because you are looking in the wrong places.'

The breeze rustled in the trees around them, and the Samdhya girl bent closer to him and explained.

The house itself was under a glamour, and the Captive was hidden in one of the layers that James had cast over it. The glamours were distorting reality. She pointed to the leaves, the life going out of them, the bleached nature of the sky.

Tom nodded in recognition. It felt, at night, when he'd gone to look, as if the house had been growing and stretching. All that energy had to come from somewhere, and James Swinton was pulling it in from the land around him.

'How do I find the right layer?'

'You have to find the glamour.' Her face took on a serious quality. 'It is not an easy task. And James is in that house. You must look without him finding out, or he will put a stop to it and work a stronger spell.' She gazed into the woods. The Samdhya never seemed to display fear, but her eyelids were twitching.

'How do I find it?'

'A glamour is anchored to an object. Find the object, and you will be able to see the glamour and find the Captive.'

'And then how do I release her?'

'I do not know how she is kept. It may be that you will need some darker magics. Or it may be that you need the help of those in the house.'

Darker magics, thought Tom. *How much darker can there be?*

'What are you?' he asked. He could not help it. They were so strange, these people, and so beautiful.

She grinned, and her teeth were uncomfortably white and sharp. Tom felt that he was in the presence of an animal. The Samdhya did not smell human, but like the wind and the trees, and their movements were fast and fluid.

'Our name – our earliest name – means the Holding Together. Let me show you.'

She closed her eyes and held out her hands as if she were drawing at a thread. In between her open palms appeared a golden structure, made up of three spheres. Each glowed with light, and each was attached to the other by a beautiful, intricate web. The spheres revolved gently; within the innermost sphere was a bright light, so bright that Tom could hardly look at it.

Tom felt as if he was looking at things beyond his comprehension. He wanted to know more, but as if in response to his unasked question, the Samdhya closed her hands together, and the structure vanished. A cloud scudded over the sun.

'We have not much time – I cannot hold you here for long,' she said.

'So I must find an object – something enchanted – and it will lead me to the Captive.'

'You have only a few days before we attack and I must make my sacrifice.'

She prepared to go.

'Wait,' said Tom. 'Your name. What is your name?'

A smile passed over her lips. 'I am called Tanenwod.'

'Tanenwod. What does it mean?'

'It means Raven in the Wood.'

She left. A brown hare, already far away. Feathers on the forest floor. A small animal skull, weathered and staring.

A few minutes later, Tom was back in his room, having reached it by the normal route, the flute in his hand, and Leana looking at him with surprise, her nose twitching and her ears pricked.

Raven in the Wood.

Ravenswood.

She was Margaret Ravenswood.

He ran to find the diary and leafed through it till he found what he was looking for. The day before her wedding. He looked again at the final entry.

He calls to me, on the wind. I hear him everywhere, when I wake, when I sleep.

I can stay here no longer.

There was one final phrase, written carefully, as if she had intended it to be read.

I am changed.

Chapter 14

*Balance is harmony. A sphere is harmony. The spheres
must balance.*

—From the Sayings of the Samdhya,
transcribed by Margaret Ravenswood

Three days before the Samdhya would attack the farm; three
days before Tanenwod would be sacrificed for the sake of
rescuing the Captive. And Tom had no further idea about
where to go or what to do, other than that there was a
beglamoured object in the house which would lead him
to the Captive.

He had to find that object first, so that Tanenwod would
not die. So that the house would not be invaded. So that
all of them would live. He imagined a set of scales, and in
the left-hand side was the suffering of the Captive, and in
the right were his life, Kit's life, Zita's life, Tanenwod's life.

'What can I do, Leana?' Tom whispered into the lurcher's
huge floppy ears. She regarded him inquisitively with her
glinting black eyes and lifted her tail, thumping it against the
floor. Then she licked him, and he pushed her away, laughing.

Tom found Kit outside, wheeling some garden rubbish in a wheelbarrow, and took him aside. Kit had been exercising the horse in the field and doing odd jobs around the grounds. His hands were muddy. The boy's silver hair glinted in the morning light, and he appeared to Tom like someone from another world, more so when he raised his head and his silver eyes shone.

Far above them a kite soared, and the light on the moat shone and rippled, the house reflected back to them.

Tom had decided. He would need Kit and Zita to distract Jack for long enough, away from the house, so he could search it thoroughly.

'Is there ever anything that needs his attention? Outside?'

The silver-haired boy put down the wheelbarrow and scratched his face with a muddy fingernail.

'I need your help,' said Tom quietly.

Kit cleared his throat. Tom saw pleading in his eyes, a terrible conflict. His lips twitched.

'Please.' Tom touched him gently on the shoulder, and Kit flinched. Then he relaxed.

'He don't trouble himself so much 'bout the land.' He wheeled the barrow onwards, continuing over his shoulder. 'Canst ask him to inspect the wards. He'll be shifted. Out of what he gazes at.'

Tom thought. 'What about his keys?'

'He don't allus wear them on his belt. Betimes he leaves them.'

It was settled. Kit would go to Jack's rooms when he'd finished his jobs in the garden, around tea time, and ask him to strengthen the wards with him. He would say that Tom was out in the woods somewhere. Once Kit'd given the all-clear, Tom would search the house. If Jack had left his keys, Kit would lean the wheelbarrow on the right side of the bridge.

'And if Jack's coming back?'

The boy smiled. 'Leana. She'll know. Take her with you. She allus knows.'

Tom clasped Kit's hand, and the boy looked at him shyly, a gentle smile illuminating his face. He went into the house with Tom and disappeared off to find Jack.

Inside, Tom remembered he had not slept and was suddenly overcome with fatigue. He made for the tea things.

Zita was there, in a silvery dress with a feather boa round her neck, mixing some herbs in a pot, and Tom explained his plan.

'I don't know how to find the object with a glamour on it, though.'

Smoothing the cloth of her dress, Zita said, 'Well, my darling, that's easy. You just have to look.'

'Don't be facetious, Zita! This is important!'

'I'm not being facetious, Tommy dearest. Look, I tell you what I'll do. I'll come with you, and then if Jack returns, I'll send myself to him. He won't know the difference – at least, he won't for as long as it will take for me to get back here.'

'You'd do that for me?'

'I'm not doing it for you, Tommy my darling. It's for all of us. We should have done it before … but …' She smoothed her hair back, and Tom saw the bracelet that Jack had placed on her wrist.

'Does it hurt you all the time?'

She nodded. 'I'm going to help you, Tommy. I'm going to help you, even though it hurts.'

'I could kiss you!'

'Well, if you must…'

She offered her cheek to him. For a moment Tom thought about grabbing her and kissing her on the mouth.

But he gave her a hug instead.

Tom's eyelids were drooping, so he made himself a strong cup of tea and waited, munching on an apple and watching through the kitchen window across the moat. The tops of the trees waving in the wind. Three silly ducks, waddling to the edge and diving in. Leana also seemed to be waiting, keeping her head up, her ears pricked, her bright eyes alive.

Soon, Tom saw Kit and Jack walking across the lawn, as they must have walked almost every day for the last few hundred years. Jack's white shirt was stark against the green; whilst Kit's customary black made his silver hair shine even brighter.

They walked as they would have done before it was a lawn even, with Jack striding ahead, and Kit half-running to keep up just behind him, trundling the wheelbarrow.

They reached the bridge. Jack shoved the gate open. Kit, without looking back, placed the wheelbarrow carefully to the righthand side.

'He's left the keys behind.'

Tom waited until the pair had crossed the bridge into the field and closed the gate, and then he and Zita sprang into action.

They took the stairs three at a time and came hurtling into Jack's rooms, Leana flowing behind them.

Zita paused for a second on the threshold and closed her eyes.

'What are you doing?'

'Sensing the glamours.'

The objects seemed more menacing than ever. The cold dead eyes of a stuffed crocodile. The glass contraption hanging from the ceiling. A dark mirror. A bowl with a pool of ink in it. Vials, some of which seemed to be full of blood, some of which contained bright liquids. Papers littered everything, many of which were covered with Jack's spidery handwriting. A framed engraving of the full achievement of the Swinton arms, with its distinctive leopard's head crest. A crystal ball with a velvet covering. Tarot cards, spread out in a pattern and in the centre of them, the Emperor card, seated on his mountain throne.

The desk seemed to be further away than it usually was. Tom found the keys in a silver bowl by the door and, trembling, went to open the top drawer where he'd seen the box.

There it was, bound in its iron bands, jewelled and impassive.

Zita looked at it for a second and then shook her head. 'That's not it,' she said. 'That's where he stores some of the Captive's powers for his own use.'

'How do you know?'

'I know, Tommy boy. Trust me.'

Frustrated, Tom placed it back in the drawer and locked it again.

'Tell me how to look.'

'I don't know, I just feel it. Reach out with your mind.' Zita shrugged her slim shoulders.

Tom did so. He sensed Zita near him, breathing gently, and could feel the warm energy that she emitted. Birdsong outside. Was that a plane, incongruous, somewhere in the sky? And not so far away, the main road leading to the market town? Disconnected images flashed through his mind: his housemaster, Fletch, capping his fountain pen. His friend, Fred, accepting a prize from the headmaster. Cricket matches.

And then, almost against his will, he started to think about his parents. As with all memories, his mother and father seemed to float in many different versions in front of his mind's eye. His mother, youthful, closing her handbag before a party. His father, gallantly holding the car door open and winking at her.

It wasn't the time to dwell on them, though, and he shifted his focus to the room itself. As Zita had said, he sent his mind out. He could feel the flows of energy in the room. He tested its boundaries. There was the door; there the window, there the desk and the iron-banded box.

Slowly, the layout and shape of the room formed itself in his mind. Each object shone with an inner radiance.

He sensed Jack's imprint on every single one of them; that dark, combative energy. On some he could feel Kit's cold, though sweeter, touch.

'What are we looking for?' In his mind he reached out to one of the glistening crystal spheres; but he was surprised when Zita pulled him back.

'Don't – don't leave any evidence.'

'Are we looking for something Samdhya?'

'Yes – if you can feel them. Something that's different, not Kit or me or Jack.'

He searched. 'I don't think it's here.'

They went upstairs. Tom remembered the last time he'd gone up, and how the house itself had seemed to throw him into confusion.

The passageway darkened as they entered the narrow attic stairway.

You almost had to crawl up the final three stairs, and then you entered the corridor.

'Seven doors,' said Tom. 'Seven now! And not much time.'

'You start that way, I'll go this.'

Tom went to the right, to the first door. It opened easily, and he came into a room, bare except for a narrow single bed, a small wooden bedside table, a curtain flapping at the open window, and, sitting on the bed, his father.

'Hello, old thing,' said his father, looking up from a newspaper. He hadn't shaved, so it must be a Saturday, and he was wearing an old grey shirt and some flannel trousers. His sleeves were rolled up. He folded the paper neatly, as he always did when Tom came to him to ask him for things, and put it aside on the bed.

'I was just reading a fascinating piece about Iran.'

'Daddy?' Tom stepped forwards into the room. Suddenly he was nine again. He felt as if he were standing on the edge of a cliff. One push and he would be over.

'What do you think we should do today, old thing? I thought we could go play some tennis? Then have some lunch in the park café? I know you like knickerbocker glories!'

'That sounds… that sounds great, Daddy.'

'Extra marshmallows, old chap!'

Tom stepped nearer to the bed. There was a hunger in his stomach and his mouth was dry. His father was here.

His father had never died, it was all a trick. This whole thing had been a trick, leading him here, to this house. His father was a Swinton, after all. This was his house as much as it was James's.

'Daddy! I'm here. I missed you.'

'And after the park maybe we'll go home and play some pool?'

Tom paused. His father wasn't responding to him as if he hadn't seen him for five years. Something else was going on. The sense of the vastness of the drop over the cliff engulfed him. Was there anything at the bottom, or was it just blackness?

'What's the matter, Tom? You look worried about something. Is it school?'

'No, Daddy, it's nothing. I'm just…'

'Why don't you come and give your old father a hug?'

Tom was about to do so, when he noticed his father's eyes.

They were not quite blue, as his father's had been. Instead they were grey, and misty wreaths passed over them. The whole figure seemed indeed to be slightly blurry at the edges, as if at any minute Tom might blow on him and send him away.

It was an apparition. A wraith.

Jack must have created it. Tom clenched his fists, his nails scoring into his palms.

'I … you're not my father.'

'What are you saying, Tom?' The apparition stood up. He noticed it was willowy now. He shouldn't have been convinced by this thing.

'You're not my father!'

Wildly, Tom prepared himself for contact as the apparition strode towards him. Putting his arms up, he closed his eyes, and a cold force slid all round him. He gathered together as much energy as he could within him, and sent it out in a huge burst.

When he opened his eyes, the apparition had gone and there was not even a newspaper on the bed.

Sadness welled up within him, but he pushed it aside. He had to stay alert and clear-headed. It was the only way.

Tom shut his eyes and focused all his attention on the objects in the room. There was the bed, there the walls, behind him the door. All he wanted now was to run out of that door and away.

But he could not.

He sent his mind out. Nothing in the room emanated any energy at all, apart from a box on the bed, which seemed to be where the apparition had come from; and that bore the mark of Jack.

When Tom opened his eyes, the apparition was back where it had been, reading its newspaper. It looked up.

'Hello, old thing,' it said, folding the newspaper and putting it aside.

Tom backed away, slammed the door shut and, panting, stood with his back against the door. Leana was on the landing.

'Any sign of him?'

The dog, as if she understood what he was asking, did not move.

He was mightily relieved when the doorknob didn't rattle.

'Zita?' he called.

He heard her answer from the room next door, and, half afraid, half nervous, he sidled in.

It was just as bare as the other, with another narrow bed, a bedside table next to it and a wooden chair on bare white boards. Tom wondered when was the last time someone had slept in any of these rooms. Cobwebs hung in the corners, and the glass on the windows was grimy.

Zita was draped across the bed, elbow propped up on a pillow, and Tom was surprised to see that she was wearing what appeared to be a nightgown. The feather boa was also wrapped around her neck, and a headband with three sleek black feathers sat on her carefully coiffed hair.

'Oh, Tommy dearest,' she said. 'You've found me a little *deshabillée*. Won't you share a cocktail with me? I've got some new recipes.'

'Now? We've got to find this thing. Any luck in here?'

'I found one called a Harvey Wallbanger. Sounds remarkable, doesn't it?'

'Zita – not now. Can you see anything in here? Is there anything in the drawer?' He rattled the handle, but there was nothing in it apart from some old bits of string and a paperclip.

'Do you think it makes you bang your head against the wall? I can't think why else they'd call it that.'

Tom was poking around in the cobwebs. Nothing.

'I promise I won't hurt you. Come, Tommy. Sit down next to me. Tell me all your secrets. You must have some. Everybody keeps something to themselves.'

Zita was still looking at him with the same demeanour. Tom went to sit next to her, and she stroked his cheek with her finger. An electric sensation passed over him.

'Zita …'

'Hush, now, Tommy boy,' she whispered. 'No need to say anything. I know what you want. My beautiful Tommy.'

The door burst open.

Framed in the doorway was Zita, the real Zita. She looked worried, and her expression changed into one of great relief when she saw Tom.

'Tommy, don't!'

He sprang away from the bed.

'You're all right!'

The apparition dissolved into shreds of mist.

'Better check this room quickly.' Tom closed his eyes, sensing the room unfold in his mind's eye; all of it was brimming with energy, but it was Jack's alone.

'Come on, I've looked at four of them. How many have you done?'

'Just two.'

'What are these things?' Tom said, as they closed the door behind them.

'Glamours of memory, of desire, all sorts of glamours. He knows what he's doing, Jack! I don't know what we'll find in the final room.'

'What was in the others? What did you see?'

Zita went pink. 'One day, darling boy, you'll be old enough for me to tell you.'

The final room was under the eaves in the western corner of the house. Leana was sitting on the landing, as motionless as a stone statue of a dog guarding a doorstep. Only the very ends of her whiskers were twitching, as if she were sensing the air. Tom wondered if the dog were as gifted as Zita and Kit.

The door, like the others, was latched. Tom lifted up the latch quietly.

They stood for a second on the threshold, and Tom found his hand grazing Zita's, and her fingers curled round his.

He and Zita went through together.

They found themselves in a darkened room. The curtains

were closed, and the window too. There was a double bed tucked into the far side, and a heavy, ancient wardrobe.

Someone was asleep on the bed, breathing quietly.

'Is that her?' Tom moved closer. 'Could that be the Captive?'

Zita looked nonplussed. 'I just … I just don't know.'

They edged nearer the bed.

Their eyes were growing accustomed to the gloom. It was strangely quiet, and Tom could not even hear the sound of traffic.

On the bed was a young man, lying on his back, in a deep sleep.

His features looked surprisingly like Tom's.

'My God,' whispered Tom. 'I can't go any closer.'

'Why not?'

'I don't know. It's like there's a forcefield around him.' Then he realised: 'It's him. It's Jack.'

Tom sent his mind out into the room.

Almost immediately he sensed something different.

It was under the bed, the gleam of something weird, untamed, pure and ancient, blocked and hedged around by powerful dark strands of Jack's energy.

Zita had found it too. They opened their eyes and stared at each other.

'Can you get nearer?'

Zita tried, but in the same way as it had Tom, an invisible barrier blocked her from nearing the bed.

'We'll need to take it apart,' she said. 'Can you feel it?'

'Yes – it's Jack. It's strong.' He felt the barrier. It was very much like the wards around the farm. 'I think I know how this works. I think I can break it apart.'

'It'll take a lot of energy.'

'I'll start.' Tom gritted his teeth and inspected the wall of energy. Here and there were little faults and bumps and knots. Jack clearly hadn't strengthened the wards around it in a while.

Gently, Tom sent out some power into one of the faults.

Almost immediately, the sleeping young man shifted, snorted, groaned in his sleep.

As if in answer, Leana started to bark, the short, sharp noise that meant someone was coming; Zita and Tom fled the room as fast as they could.

The lurcher was already waiting for them at the edge of the landing. They needed no further warning.

'Can you send yourself?'

Zita looked alarmed. 'I don't think we have time …'

Leaping down the stairs, Tom caught sight of Jack through the window, pacing back over the bridge, followed by Kit, who was dawdling as much as he was able to do so. Kit stumbled, and Jack turned irritably to help him.

Within half a minute, Tom and Zita were in the kitchen, and Zita had put an apron on, and Tom was busy peeling potatoes as if he'd been doing it for the past ten minutes.

Leana flopped down on her bed and gave a huge, blustery sigh.

'… rather a good bit, actually,' said Zita, as the door burst open. 'I've always liked Jane Austen, even the twentieth time through …' The kitchen immediately felt smaller, and Jack swept in, pausing only to glance at Zita and Tom.

'Wards are good. Good work by you, Thomas Swinton. Strong.' He glared around the room. 'Zita, I need you in my rooms. Come.'

'But I'm just telling Tom about the book I'm reading. He'll be longing to hear the end, won't you, Tommy boy?'

Tom managed to force his expression into a smile. 'Yes, I'd like to read it after Zita.' Inside he was trembling. His mouth was dry. Would Jack be able to sense that they'd been up in the attic? That they'd triggered some of his traps? Worse, that Tom had started trying to bring the wards down?

Jack left, Zita behind him. She turned and winked at Tom.

Kit, hovering in the doorway, looked at him, the question evident in his face.

'How was it?' Tom whispered.

Kit checked the kitchen door was shut and came closer to Tom. He spoke in a low voice. 'Master says the wards be strong enough.'

Tom nodded. 'I think I know where the beglamoured object is. But how to get it … that's going to be hard.'

'We maun do it, Tom. We maun.' Once more Tom was blasted by the pain and sorrow in Kit's eyes. Tom wondered when was the last time anyone had held Kit, and so he took the silver-haired boy into his arms, and soon Kit began to sob.

He wept for a long time, and when he had finished, he looked up, grateful.

'I did love him once. Master. But then he desired the Samdhya … it was more'n I could bear. It ain't right. It ain't natural. I ain't natural. I should'a been dead, in the earth, my soul wi' my God, my flesh eaten by worms.'

Leana too came to offer her sympathy and pressed her wet nose into Kit's hand.

'We'll get him, Kit. I promise you.'

'Upon thy honour?' Once more that ancient voice was coming back through, the ancient words, the glimpses of what Kit had been, so long ago.

'On my honour.' Tom squeezed Kit's hand. 'And on my mother and father.'

This seemed to satisfy Kit, and the boy stood. There was a look of gratitude in his eyes, and he straightened himself, returning to his tasks, leaving Tom alone in the kitchen, his mind spinning with plans.

Chapter 15

Our minds break through the ramparts of the universe.

— From the Sayings of the Samdhya,
transcribed by Margaret Ravenswood

When Kit had gone, Tom paced around the kitchen, making endless cups of tea and tearing at crusts of bread with his teeth, hardly bothering to spread them with butter. The afternoon light was clear, and the woods and fields outside seemed still; the horse was quietly grazing in the home field, and the water in the moat was mirror-like.

Tanenwod had told Tom not to sound the flute again. Even so, he carried it around with him in his pocket, liking the feel of its simplicity, the care that had gone into its making, liking the fact that it connected him to her. He wondered if she had used it, if some of her breath had gone into it; perhaps she had made it herself, those beautiful fingers shaping and carving the wood.

Zita appeared in the kitchen at dinner time. She seemed worn, black shadows under her eyes. Yet she still retained her impish spark, her eyes darting at Tom.

'He's asked me to make more healing draughts,' she said, nibbling at a boiled potato with a delicacy which only she was capable of. 'I think he might be worried about this attack.'

'That's good – it plays to our advantage.' Tom could not eat anything himself. His stomach was alive with nerves. 'We need to get back up to the attic, and to that room.'

'That was Jack, wasn't it? But was it Jack's actual self? Or was it a past version of himself? Or a sending? He must be very powerful if it is a sending. I'd be exhausted if I was doing a permanent sending. It takes enough out of me to do one.'

'You know more about these things than I do, Zita,' said Tom. 'I just want to know how we can get past him.'

'I'll work on it,' said Zita. 'You see what you can find too.'

'I'll have a look in the books. There might be something in Margaret's diary.'

Zita reached out and stroked his cheek. The kettle boiled and hissed, and Tom rushed to take it off. When he'd done it, she stood near him.

'This has to happen, Tommy dearest. It has to.'

Tom held her hand for a second and then released it.

In the hall, the clock struck half past seven.

A few minutes later, Tom was heading up to the library, Leana at his heels, when a rasping voice called his name.

It was Jack, of course, standing at the top of the stairs, seeming to occupy far more space than was necessary. He loomed, half in shadow, and turned on his heel.

'Thomas Swinton. Come.'

There was a command in the voice that brooked no dissent. Tom had to follow.

'It's time,' said Jack, as he sat behind his desk, 'for me to show you what you want to see. What you have always wanted to see. I have watched you, Thomas. I have seen you, wanting.'

He waited. But Tom did not answer. He did not want to let Jack know that he was right. He stood with his arms folded in front of his chest, almost as if he were hugging himself.

'You think you can play with me? Very well. But I know what it is. Your parents. The death of your parents.'

Tom remained mute. He knew he could not accept this. If he did, he would be Jack's creature, for eternity, like Zita, like Kit. He would be bound to the old man. His indentured apprentice, his bondsman.

'It is time,' said Jack, 'for me to show you who you are and what you must do.'

'Why?' said Tom. 'Why must I do it?'

Jack said, 'Turn around.'

He indicated the glass structure which was hanging from the ceiling.

'Go and look in it.'

Stumbling a little, Tom inched towards the structure. Once more he felt odd and slightly queasy when he neared it, as if it wasn't quite filling up the space it was supposed to.

'What do you see inside?'

Tom saw his own reflection, brow furrowed, eyes wide, staring back at him, and Jack behind him, glowering.

'I see myself. And you.'

'And anything else?'

In the far corner of the glass box something was fluttering. Something white and pale. Something that was forming into the shape of a person, black-haired, dark-eyed.

Tom focused fully on the form.

She came to the edge of the structure and tapped, eyes wide. They were separated by a thin sheet of glass. But by how much power?

Zita. It was Zita.

She was trapped. Trapped, inside the glass box. She spoke his name, and he could hear her, although her voice was distorted and came as if from far away.

'What have you done? Get her out!' His voice cracked.

'You touch me, Thomas, with your concern for Zita. You conceive that I am unable to know what you do when I am not here. Alas, you are wrong, indeed you are wrong. I told you she was trouble. I did not know that she would seek to betray me. You found the room with the Captive. I am not so slow nor so stupid.'

Jack grinned his devilish grin, his white sharp teeth showing like a wolf's.

'You're a monster. There's nothing human left in you!'

'Some may say so.' Jack poured himself a small glass of dark wine and sniffed it gently. 'Delicious port wine. You will not join me?'

Tom shook his head.

'Others may see what I have done and think me to be a man of genius. None have accomplished what I have.

None in all of time past. In all my travels, I have never met one like me, who has conquered time.' He took a slow sip of port. His eyes gleamed below his white brows, and Tom felt as if the entire world was collapsing around him.

Somehow, he managed to open his mouth, the words falling out in a torrent.

'It doesn't make you special. You've captured this Samdhya – you've captured Kit and Zita. You've captured me. You torture them. And who knows what you will do to me!'

'Kit loved me once. As did Zita. As, one day, may you.'

'You've destroyed Kit. Zita, too. They had lives!'

'But did you, Tommy boy? Did you have a life? Kicking around that school, wondering what to do with yourself, amongst those dreadful boys. You didn't feel happy there, did you? And what will you go back to? What does your life offer to you in the future? Some futile task, sitting in some terrible white room, staring into those vile machines?'

Jack was penetrating into Tom's mind and soul. He knew what was in there. He knew the uncertainty, the fear, the loss, the anxiety. It was true. He had been adrift. For a few days, on Mundham Farm, he had been happy, dancing with Zita, walking the bounds with Kit.

Maybe he could be happy here, with Jack and Zita and Kit. Maybe he could find happiness of a kind. There must be ways to deal with it. Jack swilled the port wine in the crystal glass.

He heard a sob from behind him. Zita. It brought him back to his senses.

'I will never love you.'

Jack put down the glass and folded his hands together, and once more Tom was struck by the brute strength in them.

'When I show you your parents, you will want to see more. You will come to appreciate what I have. The power.'

'I don't want to see them. I don't want to see my parents. You showed me my father in the attic, but it wasn't him, it was an empty thing, a wraith.'

'I will show them as they were, Thomas Swinton. And then you will belong to me.'

'I won't do it.' His heart was thumping. His tongue felt huge and thick between his lips.

'Won't you, Thomas? Won't you? If you do not come with me, think on what might happen to your friend Zita.' He pointed his long bony finger.

Tom gazed into the glass box. The silver bracelet was digging into Zita's skin so hard that she was bleeding.

'She'll die.'

'Come with me.'

'No, Tom, please!' Zita's voice, faint, was pleading.

'I will kill her if you don't.'

Tom ran to the glass box and rushed to tear it from its hooks.

'Do that and I will kill you both.'

Almost sobbing, Tom leaned his head against the cool glass, and Zita mimicked him. Their foreheads met. And for a moment the pair stood there, apparently touching, but separated by malice and an infinity of space.

Jack closed his eyes and began to mutter. The silver bracelet on Zita's wrist sank into her flesh and a single line of blood dripped down her arm.

Tom sprang back from the mirror. 'Don't! Stop it!'

'I will kill her, Thomas.'

'All right! I'll do it. I'll go with you. I'll see them.' He slumped against a bookcase.

Jack drew a deep breath, and the bracelet became loose once more.

'But I have one condition.' Tom's mind was galloping.

'You have a condition? Well, I appreciate that kind of thinking. What is it?'

'You free her. You let her go when I come back. And Kit too. You free them both. I give myself to you if you free them.'

Zita was banging on the glass, shaking her head, but Tom couldn't quite hear her.

The air was thick. Dust swirled in the sunbeams. The eyes of the stuffed crocodile glinted.

Jack put down his port glass and looked at Tom with keen eyes. 'You would do that? You would sacrifice yourself for Zita and Kit? For a wench and a serving boy?'

'They're amazing. They've served you for too long. They deserve to be free. You owe it to them!'

Jack folded his hands together, infuriatingly calm. 'Well, Thomas Swinton, you do surprise me.'

'Tommy, please, don't!' Zita's voice came from her prison, far off and strange.

Tom took one last look at Zita. She was pressed as closely as she could be against her side of the glass. He reached out and touched his fingers to her forehead, and she bowed, as if feeling the pressure. He was sure in that moment that he loved her. Sure that he had always loved her, maybe even from the moment that she had first appeared to him at school, carrying the letter.

Then Tom turned his back on her, ignoring her pleas.

'I want proof. I want proof that you'll set them free. That you'll release them. Both of them.'

'Good man. You are a Swinton after all. Well, then, you have my word as a Swinton. That is all that has ever been needed.'

'And you have mine.'

Jack reached his gnarled hand out, and Tom slowly moved towards it.

They shook hands.

Tom felt the harsh electric surge of possibility in the old man's fingers. He fought the fear in his stomach, the grim taste in his mouth. The next words he spoke were quiet but clear.

'Now. Show me.'

Jack nodded, and a glimmer of something that Tom had not seen before passed behind his eyes, like grudging respect. He glanced behind and saw that Zita had retreated, her face in her hands.

She would be free. So why was she unhappy?

Tom shuffled round to the other side of the desk, and Jack took his time finding the key, opening the drawer and taking out the iron-bound box, as if it were a rare and precious jewel.

He could not hide the look of triumph on his face.

'Put your hand on mine.' He was gloating.

Tom, resolve forming in his mind, did so. The old man's skin was rough, and Tom considered that he was holding the hand of a man who had been born in the sixteenth century.

How must he have felt, to witness the coming of electricity and motors and oil and engines? Had Jack watched in wonder when he saw the first aeroplane tearing through the clouds?

Looking at Jack, Tom sensed that he was dead inside, and that he had been dead for as long as he was able to remember. Only the past was alive for him.

Tom did not want to be like that.

And yet he had chosen.

Once more, the world changed. The dizzying sensation, the sickness, the pull in his stomach, the blackness, the elation.

Now it was light. There was a tang of salt in the air and the cry of seagulls. Sunlight beat down strongly onto a white-painted wooden deck. Ropes strained, and white sails fluttered in the wind, bellying outwards. Behind them a wake rippled across the calm ocean, blue, with darker greenish waves lapping gently. A dark shadow drifted nearby. A dolphin perhaps.

They were on a boat. All around them the sky was clear, and the edges of the sea seemed to merge with the sky.

'This is the boat. *The Wanderer*. They're here.' Tom ran from Jack, stumbling towards the stern.

His mother was steering, a look of calm concentration on her face. His father was poring over a map.

'What do you think he's doing right now?' said his mother. She scratched the side of her nose in that way that she had. She was sunburnt and smiling and her hair was noticeably lighter. She wore a black-and-white striped T-shirt, and white shorts that were now looking a bit grubby and frayed. A bottle of water was close to hand.

His father looked up and smiled. 'He's probably just coming out of lessons. The bell's ringing, he's running out for break before lunch time.'

'Do you think he's happy?' She swigged her water.

'I hope so, my darling. We'll be seeing him soon. We're over halfway now.'

Tom realised with a sudden lurch of love that they were talking about him.

He reached out to touch her shoulder, but he found he could not make contact.

Jack was standing by him.

'You cannot touch them. You cannot change things. You cannot warn them.'

Warn them.

Tom turned back to watching them. Perhaps it was enough just to be here, to see them.

He thought about the future. He would come here again and again. Perhaps he could come here every day, and watch them, and memorise the patterns of freckles on their faces, the colours in their irises. Perhaps he could stay here always, just watching them, listening to them talking to each other over and over again, until he knew their final moments by heart.

His father reached out to stroke a hair away from his mother's face.

'Fighting a losing battle there,' joked his mother.

Tom remembered what he had been doing on the day they had died. It was as clear in his mind as if it had happened an hour ago. It had been a history lesson, the year before he'd gone to Downshire College, at his boarding prep school. They'd been studying the Crusades. Richard the Lionheart.

The school secretary had come to get him to bring him to the headmaster's study. He remembered she'd been fiddling with her glasses round her neck and that she'd been particularly hushed.

At first he had thought that he'd done something wrong, but then, as she led him through the school towards the Victorian house where the headmaster lived, and he was taken into the headmaster's own private rooms, where a stuffed pheasant sat in a glass case on a mantelpiece, there was the growing realisation that something terrible had happened. The matron was sitting there, hands folded in her lap, hardly able to look at him when he came in. The headmaster, standing, waiting for him. He'd knelt down on the carpet, to be on his level, and Tom remembered noticing his trousers riding up his shins.

Those words, passing in a blur. 'I'm so sorry, Thomas. I'm afraid there's been an accident.'

The tears. The hot chocolate given to him by the matron, the blankness of the evening, spent in the sick room, with the headmaster's wife and the matron sitting alternately with him through the night.

The looks, the next day, from the rest of the boys and girls.

'I'm getting some strange readings, William.' His mother was frowning over the radar.

Tom's father looked up and went over to the controls. 'That looks like a storm coming on.'

'It's odd – there was nothing in the weather report.' She pressed the button on the radio system. 'It's not working.'

'Weird.'

The sky darkened. A powerful wind began to blow, as if from nowhere, and the boat rocked violently, sending cold spray across the decks.

Tom, even though he knew that he could not be harmed, grabbed on to a rope.

'Can't you change it?' he said to Jack, who was looking on with imperturbable calm.

Jack shook his head. 'Nothing can be changed.'

A wave crashed over the bows, drenching Tom's mother and father. The boat pitched violently from side to side.

Above them was now almost entirely dark, and the rain was hurtling down as harshly as hail. A sudden fork of lightning illuminated the boat, and Tom saw his mother and his father clutching each other.

'Lifejackets!'

'Take me away.' Tom clutched at Jack. 'Take me away, I don't want to see, I don't…'

'You will remember their faces.'

'I don't want to remember them like this.'

Tossing from side to side, the boat was now at the top of a huge wave, and his parents slipped, grabbing on to the railings for support. Thunder crashed. Tom was almost blinded by the rain.

'Take me away!'

Jack laughed, and Tom remembered his laughter for a long time, even as he stood back in Jack's rooms, and tumbled, blindly, into a chair, it rang still in his ears.

Light striped the wooden floor. Tom saw the paraphernalia of Jack's rooms as if it were veiled by a membrane. Something was trying to break through the skin. He remembered. Dark, carefully coiffed hair. Deep eyes. Silver eyes.

Kit. Zita. He'd asked Jack for their freedom.

He sat up straight and focused ahead of him. Jack was sitting behind his desk, with his arms behind his head, regarding Tom with questioning, hungry eyes.

'Free them. Free them now.' It was all he could get out.

'Look behind you, Thomas Swinton.'

Tom did so, slowly. There was the glass box.

171

There was Zita, still imprisoned.

And there, beside her, was Kit.

'I have no need of them now,' said Jack.

'I asked you to free them!'

'They are free from my influence now. They can do as they wish. You did not specify what you wished for them. Now you will do what they did. You would always have performed the tasks better than they.'

It was impossible. He was trapped inside the house. Jack would kill Zita and Kit if he defied him.

He stood in a patch of sunlight between shadows.

There was nothing he could do.

Chapter 16

Time has no end and no beginning.

> —From the Sayings of the Samdhya,
> transcribed by Margaret Ravenswood

Outside the sun was high, the air humid, the sky cloudless. In other circumstances it would have been a beautiful day. After he'd seen his parents on the boat, Tom had run to his room and had managed to sleep. Now it was morning, and Jack had taken Tom out to do the wards. And Tom was compelled to follow.

The shadows of the trees fell like spears on the lawn, and rank weeds tumbled in the unkempt fields. Tom tried to imagine being at school on such a day: the noise of balls hitting cricket bats in the background, the shouts from the tennis courts, the chatter on the stairs, the boys loafing about in the quads, dawdling on their way to lessons.

But he could not hold on to the thoughts, and they slipped away as if made of smoke.

It was as if Jack and the farm and his parents had become so huge in his mind now that these were the only things it could contain. Tom walked, treading slowly, watching his feet, looking up only when Jack needed him.

Jack was a silent companion.

They tramped around the boundaries of the farm, making sure that the wards were as strong as possible. They saw nothing, not a single squirrel on the trees, nor a kite above, yet still Tom felt that all the time eyes were fixated on him.

Whenever they stopped to shore up the farm's protections, Tom sensed Jack's dark energy oozing out and mixing with his own. It made him feel ill. He was exhausted, but his mind was still whirring, always nagging at the same question. How could he stop this? He needed to prevent the Samdhya from attacking; free Kit and Zita, and put an end to Jack's reign of terror once and for all.

And yet now, here he was, Jack's henchman, and probable successor.

He wondered if soon he might become like Jack. How long did it take? One year, two? How long before all life and love were squeezed out of him? How long before he became a husk?

Sometimes Jack would stop and simply stare into the distance. Tom wondered what he was looking at. Was he reaching into his own mind? Was he pushing out beyond, into the world of the Samdhya? Or even into some other, deeper place?

Tom ate lunch on his own in the kitchen, placing roughly hewn slices of cheese in between some stale bread. He did not know where Jack went, and did not want to ask.

He wondered now if he would be allowed to take the cart down to the shops for food; if, like Kit, a glamour would be placed on his tongue so that he could not speak to anybody, or tell them what was happening.

As Tom was washing up, Jack reappeared. Tom could not help but be impressed by his presence. The white hair, the gaunt features, the strange beauty.

But also the eyes, the blackness in them, the heartlessness.

'You'll be doing Zita's work now. I expect you'll do it better'n she.'

He opened a wooden chest which stood under the window, and showed him the rows of carefully labelled herbs in pots and the vials of dark liquids. There was a small, handwritten book, in which Zita, in gentle, schoolgirlish handwriting, had written down the ingredients for her draughts.

Tom watched Jack as, with the care of a surgeon, he measured and crushed and poured, showing him how to mix healing draughts as Zita had done. The scents from the herbs were delicate and sweet, like freshly cut mint or grass on a summer's day.

'This one heals anything the Samdhya hit us with. This is for flesh wounds.'

Tom did not mind the work, mixing, weighing and sorting the herbs, flowers and mosses, boiling them up and pouring them off carefully into vials. There were some odd ingredients: a pheasant's feather, which Jack used to stir something, and then burned carefully. Jack was brusque, to the point, but remarkably patient if he made a mistake.

Tom understood that this was because they had to be made in the right way. Care was all. The smells, rich and earthy, reminded him of Zita, and his hands trembled as he worked.

At about six o'clock, he realised with a stab of hunger that they had been working for several hours without a break. Jack was possessed of a curious energy, which shone in his eyes and kept him moving like an automaton.

'Do you think they will be able to beat us? To break through into the farm?'

Jack looked up, and Tom saw a flicker run through his eyes. It could not be fear, but it might have been anticipation. More than anything Tom was reminded of a lizard, ageless and implacable, waiting at the crossroads for something to happen. He shuddered, half expecting a forked tongue to flicker out of his mouth.

'They are ancient and wily. They may be able to enter. Whether they will be able to break through to the Captive is another thing. I have many ways of stopping them.' Jack counted the vials of draughts carefully and placed them in their right positions.

And that was when the idea came to Tom. If he could persuade Jack to show him how the spells worked, how the defences were made, then would he also be able to pull them apart?

The thought made him pause in his work, and Jack eyed him. 'What ails you?'

'Nothing.' He scrambled for an excuse. 'I was just thinking about how to stop the Samdhya reaching the Captive.'

Tom felt the beam of Jack's eyes raking through his soul.

'We've done enough for today.' Jack rose abruptly, then slowly cleaned his hands over the sink, dried them off. 'You will come to my rooms later. I will show you your parents again.' Without looking back, he stomped out and up to his rooms.

As if from nowhere, Leana appeared and nuzzled her head onto Tom's knees. Tom gratefully tickled her chin, and then gulped down two long glasses of water, before scouring the larder. He found some stale biscuits and ate them greedily. There were some tins, which he would open later for supper.

Once he was satisfied, he thought about what he could do. He was in realms undreamed of. Nothing he had read or done at school or anywhere else could help him. All he had was the wooden flute in his pocket and the diary of Margaret Ravenswood.

Jack must have a weak spot. He must do. There must be some way that Tom could get behind his defences.

He trudged up to his room, Leana at his heels, and flung himself onto the bed. There was no mobile phone signal, of course.

A thought struck him. Perhaps he could go to the mound and find some signal there. He could call Fletcher, ask him to send someone, or even come himself, though the thought of Fletcher striding up the gravel path, bellowing in his nasal tones, seemed absurd, his ancient Ford on the drive behind him.

A few minutes later he was trudging through the long grass in the field to the west of the farm. He went past the shed with the rusting tractor in it. The horse – he had forgotten about the horse. He paused to make sure he had food and water, and that the stable was clean. The whiskery, warm breath made him feel better, and he let him out to exercise, filling up his bucket. From far off he heard dogs barking.

Underneath the trees, Leana kept close to him. The path to the mound had not been mowed in years, and Tom could barely make it out, but he stumbled through the undergrowth, falling once over a log and scraping his palms.

The mound suddenly loomed ahead of him. It was covered in grass, and waving wildflowers, and Tom began to scramble up it. Something seemed to get into the lurcher, and she started looping madly around it, running up and down in zigzags as if chasing invisible prey.

Tom reached the top. He could see the wood stretching out on either side of him, and to the east, he could just about make out the top of the farmhouse, and to the north, the comforting sight of the weathervane on top of the church spire.

He took his mobile phone out. Then he shook it in frustration. The signal bar was still empty. Not only was there none but the phone's screen began to shimmer and glitch. There was nothing, no link to the outside world.

He had not felt so alone since he had been at school at the end of the holidays. He turned the phone off and put it away. Behind him was the farm, and Jack, and all his horror. And he could not escape.

In despair, he knelt down on the top of the mound.

The flute, with its carved hare's head, was warm in his pocket. Maybe now was the time to play it. It seemed right, standing here on the mound, with Leana at his side and the trees waving in the breeze. What did he have to lose? The Samdhya might come and take him away. He might even, he thought crazily, become one of them, like Margaret Ravenswood.

It came easily to his hand, almost as if it wanted to be there, and as he put it to his lips, he sensed the life of the tree it had come from. It might almost start to sprout leaves, he thought. He blew gently through it, allowing a slow, gentle melody to disperse on the breeze, four simple notes, rising up and then sinking, and then again, and again, as if it were a hymn, or a mantra, or a call.

The shadow of a hawk passed over him. In the far fields, the long grass rustled, as if a deer were running away.

Silently seeming to melt out of the air, standing round him in a circle bristling with sharp bronze spears and swords, the Samdhya appeared.

Tom knew that if he moved he would be killed. He could not see Tanenwod anywhere, but in front of him was Rohenga. He wore a circlet of red feathers on his head, and a long earring which looked like a tooth.

The Samdhya seemed, though their mouths were not moving, to be talking amongst themselves, in a whispering, discordant buzzing.

Rohenga said nothing, but stepped forwards so that he was within a pace or two of Tom, and slowly unsheathed the jewelled dagger from his belt. He ran his finger along the edge, and then brought the point of it to Tom's gut.

'I have used this before on you.'

'I have the mark still. You did not cut me deep.'

'It was a warning. You did not heed it.' His voice was full of rough, harsh sounds, half hissing.

'You're afraid of me.' Tom did not know what he was saying. He had nothing to lose. 'You're afraid I'll become like him. That I'll keep your companion prisoner for eternity. You know Jack won't last for ever, and you know I could be like him. I could be worse than him.'

'You are a boy.'

'Jack was a boy once too.'

Rohenga scowled. 'I used to watch him in the woods. He gathered darkness even then. He was born with darkness in his heart. I saw him take a fawn and break its skull when he was a stripling. You are different. You have softness within you. I saw it near the school. I see it now. You shine like a beacon.'

'How do you know? How do you know I won't just go back to him, go back to the farm and help him defeat you? We have the Captive still. And you would not let anything happen to her.'

Rohenga, still snarling, stood aside and said, 'Tanenwod.'

Two Samdhya brought her, carrying her between them. She was not chained, but she seemed unable to move. Her eyes, deep and bright, stared at Tom. He had never seen such sadness.

'We are preparing her for her death.'

'How can you kill one of your own?'

'When the situation demands it, then it is necessary. We are the Holding Together. We are the Storm, the Deep and the Wildmark. Your kin, James Swinton, disturbs the joins. He is a dark force, tearing into the gaps, breaking things apart. Tanenwod became Samdhya. She was not born one of us.' Rohenga took a step nearer towards Tom.

'How is that different? She is like you.'

'She has no Samdhya blood. I turned her, I gave her my life force. When she dies, it will be part of me that goes.'

'But she will go too.' Tom spoke with as much conviction as he could muster.

The rustling sound became louder. Tom suddenly felt as if a thousand insects were crawling all over his skin, and he pushed down the urge to scratch himself. This was a test. He had to pass it.

'You would try to order Rohenga, the Wildlord?'

'I'm not trying to order anybody. I don't want you to kill Tanenwod.'

'Do you love her? We know of love. Love is part of the Holding Together. Not all of it, but a small part of it.'

Tom felt his face burn. Was that how he thought of Tanenwod? She stared at him, and he saw nothing human in her eyes, but instead something brutal and dark.

'We will kill her. We will kill her tonight, and we will swarm into your stronghold, and we will kill you and James Swinton.'

Tom threw himself at the Samdhya holding Tanenwod. They were so strong, the tall dark-haired one lifted him up with one arm. He heard the sound of a sword being drawn out of a sheath.

'I love them all. Zita. Kit. Tanenwod. I love them all.' Tears sprang from his eyes and wet his cheeks. 'I love them all!'

Chapter 17

Song in trees, light on water. These are the least and the greatest of things.

— From the Sayings of the Samdhya,
transcribed by Margaret Ravenswood

Hundreds of eyes and spears, all glittering in the early evening light around Tom. Tom prepared himself. He thought of his parents and how much he loved them. He thought of love, and that gave him a peace he had not felt for a long time, and he closed his eyes and focused on it; it seemed to come from somewhere further than his own mind and to fill everything around him.

'I'm ready.' He paused and opened his eyes. 'Do what you want.'

Grunts and murmurings from the crowd. 'Do you mean that, Thomas Swinton? Do you mean that, whelp of a monster?'

'He's nothing to me! Nothing! You don't understand.'

Steeling himself, Tom forced himself not to cry, staring at the Samdhya as they gathered around him, their eyes shining, their weapons threatening. He prepared himself, not caring now, not caring if they killed him.

A change came over Rohenga. The dark scowl left his brow and a smile creased over his face, and he laughed, deeply. Its sound was incongruous in the wood. The tattooed leopard on his cheek seemed to dance.

'Put him down.' Rohenga's voice was unexpectedly gentle. The tall dark-haired Samdhya placed Tom gently onto the grass. He gasped in relief. Leana came to him, flowing through the legs of the Samdhya like smoke, and licked his hand. He let his fingers brush against her whiskers.

'I see that you are true. You are nothing like him. Then, Thomas, we need you.'

Tom was astonished. 'You need me? But I...I don't know anything.'

'The ways of the world are strange and unknowable, Thomas. But some things always remain true. A stone will fall in water. A flame will burn a tree. And one of those is that it can only be a Swinton who can defeat James. That is what he knows. That is why he keeps you close now that you are of age.'

'You mean he doesn't want me to take over from him?'

Rohenga clenched his teeth and sighed. 'He wants to kill you.'

It had been a trap. The whole thing. He had been led here, by Zita, to his death.

'You must go now. If you can do it, do it now. Go to the house. Find the Captive. Break James Swinton's power.

Break his power so that you survive. Break his power so that everything survives.'

The Samdhya shook their spears, making a low thudding sound as they pounded the soft ground.

'You told me he was breaking things…'

'He has some power we do not understand.'

'How can I do this on my own? You won't attack the house? You gave us three days. I thought you were working out how to defeat him.'

Rohenga smiled, showing white teeth and sharp canines. 'You were right. We have found the Knot. But we will not use it.'

'You made me think you might.'

'It was a threat, to frighten James Swinton, to see if we could find a gap in his defences whilst he strengthened them.'

'And did you?'

A look of dark sorrow came over Rohenga's face. 'We cannot. His power is too dark, too savage. The house is him, he is the house, he is the wards. His mind is vast and ancient and deep, and he has seen more than any man should see. But these are things for another time.' He looked towards the house. 'We also wished to test you. To see if you were of his kind.'

'I'm not strong enough. I don't know how to release the Captive.'

It was impossible. Everything was impossible. He felt the weight of expectation on him, almost alive, rising from the ranks of the Samdhya. He could hardly believe it.

These dangerous, powerful creatures wanted him to help them.

'You will find a way.'

'That's not enough – how can I find a way? I barely understand what I do when I make the wards.'

'You *must* find a way. And then you must bring the Captive over the water.'

'I have to bring her myself?'

'A Samdhya can only cross the water if carried by a mortal.'

The two Samdhya guarding Tanenwod had released her, and now she stood, proud and tall. A second later, she vanished, and in her place was a hare, whiskers twitching, which, after a moment's gleam of her eyes, bounded away.

'Who is the Captive?'

'She is of us and above us. She is the least and the greatest of us. She is Song in Trees, Light on Water.'

It all felt impossible. 'I can't … I don't know what to do.'

A sickness gathered in Tom's stomach, like a heavy stone. His nerves seemed to be clogging up his throat.

'Tanenwod will watch. If you need her, play the flute, and she will do what she can.'

Rohenga reached out and grasped Tom by the shoulder, showing his pointed white teeth. At any moment, Rohenga might strike, or fly away. But the stately, dark-eyed Samdhya smiled, and looked away from Tom. 'I must not look at you too long. You do not wish to be one of us.'

There was a rustling, like leaves in the breeze, and instead of the Samdhya, Tom was surrounded by animals. Red stags with branching antlers, gentle does, a badger's white stripe in the dark, the eyes of rats and hedgehogs and squirrels and jays and ravens, everywhere, on every branch and covering the ground all around him. Then, as if at a signal unheard, they were gone, and all Tom could see was a rabbit's white scut, away into the distance.

The journey back passed as if he were in a dream. Leana had bounded on ahead. Tom barely saw his feet, his mind focused on one thing only, reaching for it, rubbing at its edges, the dark, hard, hopeless task that lay ahead of him.

The ridged top of the farmhouse appeared through the trees, and he stood looking at it. Its boundaries blurred. Once more it seemed to shift into a different kind of house, turreted and impregnable. Then the illusion disappeared and the farmhouse returned to its solid form.

He had to think clearly. He had to face up to Jack now. He had to find the Captive, release her.

The short sword that Zita had given him. He went stealthily into the kitchen. The remains of his lunch were still on the table and the draughts that he had had to make. He tucked a few of them into his pockets, hoping they would come in useful. Then he spooned the contents of a tin of tuna into his mouth, washing it down with water. The sword, he remembered, was hanging in the hall, in a small alcove. The door into the main hall was closed.

He opened it quietly and peered inside. It was shadowy and cool and empty. Tom listened for footsteps, but could hear none. Jack must be in his rooms, he surmised, floating throughout time, watching Brutus kill Caesar, perhaps, or the Great Wall of China being built or the first human awakening into consciousness.

The sword was where he had left it. He took it carefully from its hooks, lifting it easily upwards. It was in an unprepossessing sheath made from tough leather, and an obviously ancient, well-worn leather belt went with it. Girding himself, he felt suddenly ridiculous. He had never used a sword before. What on earth was he meant to do with it now? But the thought of it gave him strength, even though he was not sure he would be able to harm Jack with it.

The stairs loomed. The corners seemed further away, the height greater, shadows spilling where there should be no shadows. The hairs on the back of Tom's neck and arms began to bristle, and an unpleasant shiver passed over him.

Tom paused at the bottom, and a clock chimed, startling him. He had lost all sense of time. It was eight o'clock. He put his hand to the banisters. What might bring Jack away from his travels in the web of time? Carefully, Tom trod up the steps as softly as he was able.

The first-floor landing was dark. Tom was glad that Jack's rooms were the furthest away from the stairs. He pressed his back against the wall and edged carefully upwards. The sword clanked uncomfortably.

Reaching the attic landing, he found it normal. The door to the seventh room was firmly closed. Tom steeled himself and, gripping the sword handle, went inside.

He blinked.

Ahead of him, instead of the small attic room he had been expecting, was a wide, spacious chamber, panelled with dark oak and richly furnished, tapestries hanging on the walls, gilt-framed pictures and well-upholstered chairs. A beautifully carved chess set stood on a table, although there seemed to be more pieces than were usual, and some of them Tom could not name. There was a smell of fresh polish and in a glass vase was a spray of gorgeous white and blue flowers that looked like nothing he had ever seen in the fields or woods.

Tom checked over his shoulder. The corridor was the same as it had been.

Feeling a little uncertain, he stepped back into the large wood-panelled space. The tapestries hanging on the walls glowed with rich reds and golds and greens. The designs were sometimes geometric, sometimes figurative.

As he stared at them, they took on a greater meaning, and for half a second he felt like he was on the edge of some immense truth. But almost as soon as he thought he had grasped it, it slipped away, leaving him gasping in disappointment.

The room was long and rectangular, and at the other end of it was another door, decorated with gold, an inscription above it in a language Tom did not recognise but which he immediately understood.

A shadow comes from light.

He went, half-running, to the gilded door, and tried the handle, and stepped through into another long room, almost identical to the one he had just left. The walls were leafed with silver and lined with weapons. A huge axe hung menacingly over a mantelpiece. Swords, crossed against each other, were suspended above shields with animals embellished on them. A mace, with a terrifying spiked ball at the end of a chain, looked like it might crush somebody's skull with ease.

Tom stood in awe in front of a spear so heavy it would need a giant to heft it. He reached out to pick up a small jewelled arrowhead, and as he did so, he heard the sound of a door opening and he looked up to see a man entering from the other end of the room.

Almost immediately Tom stiffened. He knew this man. He was wearing a black high-peaked hat with a white feather in it, a black doublet and a white ruff, and white lace spilled from his sleeves like froth. From his left ear hung a diamond on a black ribbon.

It was the younger version of Jack Swinton, whom he'd seen sleeping in the attic.

Young Jack regarded Tom with a critical eye.

'You have reached this far.' He doffed his plumed cap and placed it on a table next to a sword in a jewelled scabbard. 'You arrive armed.'

'Who are you?' Tom swivelled sideways so that the long heavy table was in between him and Young Jack. 'What are you?'

'James Swinton.'

'But he's ancient. You're …'

'I ain't. Curious, is it not? I am still he. I have long inhabited these halls, which exist in a crystalline sphere encircling the terrestrial. I know little else. But there are so many worlds to discover. You saw the tapestries? She makes 'em.'

'The Samdhya?'

'She weaves 'em, imparting her knowledge into the threads. I know all their innermost secrets. The dark recesses of their knowledge. I have spoken with airy spirits and seen into the spheres of the cosmos.' His face shone with passion.

'What are they? The Samdhya?' Tom was trying to position himself so that he could flee through the door behind him.

Young Jack picked at the lace on his cuffs. 'They are not like us. They have been here always, and yet they tread the ways between worlds. They think that they protect us. Some might think that they keep us in ignorance.' With sudden, balletic speed, he lifted up a small throwing spear and, leaning back a little onto his right foot, he hurled it with full force at Tom.

Some deep instinct made Tom duck, and the spear passed within a handspan of his shoulder. He peered at Young Jack, trembling. The most extraordinary smile was on his face, and his eyes were lit with malice. Tom felt for his sword. He had no idea how to use it.

There was no way that Tom could get past him. Yet he could not go back and face Old Jack. There was only one thing he could do.

He would have to fight.

Young Jack sneered. For a moment his face was contorted in pure evil, and fear shivered its cold tendrils down Tom's spine.

'You are too weak to pass me.' His adversary casually took the mace from its hooks and, lifting it, brought it down on the edge of the table, which shattered into splinters.

As quickly as the mace seemed to fly back upwards, Tom remembered what Rohenga had said to him in the wood. *You will find a way.* Was it the sword? He half-pulled it out.

Jack smirked at him. 'I see you have no knowledge of the sword. Then…' He started forwards in a feint.

The only way he had was what Zita had shown him. He sensed the energy in the room, the power. All around him were the wild traces of the Captive. Young Jack radiated the black force he knew so well and hated so much. Gently, he reached out with his mind and touched the edges of the Samdhya energy and pulled it into himself. The room was glowing and glimmering

It filled him with new strength. Weaving as much of the Samdhya energy as possible into his own, he moulded it into a ball of furious power and propelled it at Young Jack, smashing it right into his stomach and forcing him to bend double at the waist.

'A hit,' gasped Young Jack. His knees were buckling, he crumpled, and Tom dashed towards the door.

A fraction of a second later, Young Jack straightened and drew his arm back, and the full force of a dark blast smashed

Tom onto a crimson rug. He rolled over and jumped back upwards, crouching low to regain his energy.

He reached out once more to the traces of the Samdhya. But something was wrong. Young Jack was blocking him.

A heavy thump sounded to his left. The mace landed just by him. Tom scrambled back on his heels and slammed into Young Jack with a raging pulse.

Young Jack staggered backwards and dropped the mace. He was trembling now. Tom withdrew his sword from his scabbard and made a dash for the door. Just before he reached it, his adversary drew himself up and threw one final burst of power at Tom.

But Tom deflected it, meeting it with his own.

He reached the door.

'You will not succeed.' Young Jack, sunk to his knees, gasped. 'The Captive is bound with such power as you do not, cannot understand. You are a pawn. You are nothing. You and the others will die. I, James Swinton, will live. I will live longer than the powers that beset us now. I will be the last.'

It was enough. All Tom's hatred of Jack and his love for Zita and Kit and his parents burst through him into a torrent of fiery power. He towered over Young Jack, feeling the strength grow within him. It was like lava. Young Jack smirked.

Then Tom struck.

This time the blow knocked Young Jack to the far side of the room, sapping Tom so much that his knees weakened and he had to grab on to the door handle for support.

The edges of his enemy began to blur. As if he were made from nothing but smoke, Young Jack began to dissolve into atoms.

But still he laughed, and the laughter rang in Tom's ears. 'You will be nothing.'

It was the last thing Tom heard before he struggled with the golden handle to the next room and pushed through.

And there, without even time to draw breath, he saw what he had been fearing.

The deck of his parents' boat. *The Wanderer*. Storm clouds were swiftly gathering overhead, spilling out from the centre of the sky, spreading across the blue expanse.

No land in sight. No ship in sight.

His father, bent over a map. His mother, trying the dials on the radio. It was 2.47pm, a mere two minutes before they drowned.

He would have to face it.

The day of the storm.

He closed the door firmly behind him and went onto the deck, the cold saltwater stinging his cheeks.

Chapter 18

A stone will fall through water. A flame will burn a tree.

—From the Sayings of the Samdhya,
transcribed by Margaret Ravenswood

A large white-tipped wave loomed from the darkening swell
and crashed over the bows. It retreated, leaving behind three
or four tiny silver fish struggling on the deck and a piece
of seaweed that dragged a freezing tendril over Tom's face.

Tom clutched at the nearest rope for support. The cold
air enveloped him, the rain, pelting down now, flattening
his hair, seeping into his mouth. A great fork of lightning
slashed right through the sky and was followed almost
immediately by an infernal rumbling of thunder.

His parents were tough, lean and wiry, having eaten only
ship's rations for a week. Yet suddenly they looked small
and vulnerable.

'I don't understand it!' His mother was shouting. 'It's
come from nowhere!'

'Nothing on the radar? Nothing on the reports?'

'Nothing! It's like it just came from above.'

'Like an act of God.'

Another vast, gloomy wave poured over the deck, drenching them in saltwater.

When it washed away, they were hanging on grimly, Tom's mother to the side of the boat, his father to the boom, which he'd managed somehow to grab.

'Take in the sails!'

They righted themselves, and struggled to do so, as the ship tossed from side to side. Tom watched in horror, wishing he could help.

'We'll get through this.'

His mother and father clung to each other. Another sharp fork of lightning ripped through the clouds, illuminating everything for a brief and appalling second, before the thunder rolled around once more. The boat was pitching about on a wave as if it were nothing but a piece of flotsam.

The storm had come from nowhere. Nothing had detected it. No instrument was able to sense its coming.

A familiar blackness spread through Tom's mind. Above him in the clouds was a force, malign and ancient. Tom recognised it. In the centre of the storm was a black, swirling disc.

This was the storm. This was what was controlling the weather. This was what had caused everything and the death of his parents.

It was Jack. His ancestor, James Swinton.

The force of the realisation hit him harder than a wave. Battered, he knelt, water sluicing over him, rain slashing at him, his parents now clinging for their lives to the mast.

His father was trying to put a lifejacket on his mother. He pulled it over her, and they kissed. She helped him on with his own and tightened the straps.

'We'll get through this.'

'Tommy. What if we don't…?'

'He'll know we loved him.'

James Swinton had made the storm.

There was a terrible creaking noise, and the boat was suddenly overturned, and Tom was plunged into the freezing depths of the ocean.

He saw, falling, their orange lifejackets, the bodies of his parents, and a terrible sadness overcame him. The storm plunged them deep down into the ocean, further than they should have gone. Dark shapes flowed and surged around them.

He fell with them.

He should stay here, with them, be with them as they died. He did not need to live. What point was there?

Another voice in his mind countered this.

No, it said. *Don't let him win. This is what he wants. He wants you to give in to despair.*

The grief slowly changed into anger.

He realised that he could move. His parents were floating back up to the surface, drowned within seconds. He wanted to throw himself at them. But he knew it would make no difference. He had something else to face now.

With a great effort, he pulled himself to the surface and saw above him the centre of the storm, radiating out from a black disc that he knew was an emanation of James Swinton.

He was shivering, with fear, cold and grief. A wave engulfed him, and he swallowed some seawater, gasping for air.

It's not real, he told himself. *It's not real. It's his mind that's making this happen.* It was James Swinton making him believe that he was cold. James Swinton making him believe that he was trapped.

Experimentally, as he trod water, he imagined warmth spreading through his body.

He started with his stomach and heart. Like a rich, warm soup, he felt it slowly spreading through his body, pushing itself to his limbs and right into his fingertips. He wiggled them. He found he could move easily, though the sea was strong.

He was now directly underneath the black disc. If the storm had come from it, he wondered if it was also a portal.

He had to reach it. Could he move through the air? Was it possible?

He looked upwards, and imagined a flow of energy coursing through him, pushing him up. Rain pounded his face. *I am not feeling this*, he thought. *The rain is an illusion.*

And it passed. Then it redoubled itself, and suddenly he was floundering again.

Not this time, he thought. He gathered himself together, gasping once more for air and steadying himself. He found a solid point and forced himself to stay there. *Now.*

Through the fierce rain he forced himself up into the sky, and suddenly he was in the air, and he felt the wind rushing over him, and the sea was beneath him, the upturned boat, the floating lifejackets, through the air onwards towards the source of the storm, towards the source of everything that had ruined his life, reaching upwards and upwards, the hull of the boat now tiny and remote, the bodies of his parents bobbing, face down, below him.

He had to reach the black disc, the terrible emptiness, the horror.

It felt like an age. He lost concentration, his body slipping back into numbness.

No, he thought. *No.*

Then he was at the edge of it, and something was pulling at him, pulling him through. The edge of it was there, it was just a hole, a hole into something strange and terrible. He scrambled onto something like solidity, and then he was through.

He did not fall. He simply stumbled, and then he was upright.

He was dry. He patted himself. He was alive, whole.

The noise of the waves and the thunder had gone. He had a moment to look about, but he did not recognise where he was.

The sudden silence was unbearable.

A room, another room, almost bare of ornament, with white walls and nothing on them, wooden floorboards, and, standing with his back to him, the looming black figure of James Swinton, and behind him, a mirror, in which Tom could see James's face.

At first Tom was struck with terror. A paralysing numbness spread through him. But then, as James smiled, the numbness left him and was replaced with a vitalising anger.

'You did it!' The words were clear in Tom's mind, the horror of them so large it felt as if he were spitting out stones. 'You killed my parents! Monster!'

With a roar of unbearable rage, Tom threw himself at Jack, beating at him with his fists.

He did not reach his target. He was hurtled backwards by an invisible wall of protection, landing on his back with a hideous thump that rattled his bones.

Jack faced Tom. He looked younger, stronger, almost like Young Jack, almost like Tom's father, almost like Tom himself. 'And why do you think I killed your parents, Thomas Swinton?' His hands were clasped in front of him. He looked so unperturbed, so calm. With one of his hands he gently began to stroke the velvet of his sleeve. His eyes were distant.

'I needed you to have nothing left.' Jack smiled, his lizard eyes dark. 'Everything you loved has gone. You have no other way.'

Tom's energy was ebbing away from him. He propelled himself once more at Jack, but the force of the rebound was too great; he fell, sobbing, to the floor.

Looming over him now was Jack. 'There is no use in your resistance. Give way. Give way to me, Thomas Swinton, last bearer of your name, last bearer of my name.'

As he rose into a crouching position, Tom felt something in his pocket. It was a flask, full of the healing draught he'd made. He pulled it out, drew the stopper with his teeth and, in two gulps, drained it.

Warmth and strength rushed through him. Zita's smile flashed before his mind. He watched Jack.

He waited.

Jack was now pacing along the other side of the room. Tom knew that he would come round the square, back to where Tom was crouching. A few paces more. Jack was singing something slowly to himself. Two more paces. One.
Now.

Tom launched himself at Jack, and burst through his wards, feeling them shattering around him like tiny pieces of glass lacerating his skin.

For a flicker of a second, Jack's face showed surprise. Tom took advantage of the momentary weakness. He could take him now. The sword was out, its point so near to Jack that he could pierce him within a moment.

'Thomas, my boy… you would kill your uncle?'

There was something so suddenly frail about Jack that Tom paused, the sword-tip poised half an inch away from Jack's stomach.

Tom hesitated.

Surging forwards, Jack pinned Tom by the throat against the wall. Those cold, strong fingers closed around his neck. The eyes, obsidian, furious, glimmering with dense fire.

His parents' killer, the dark magician.

Tom choked. He had lost. He was going now to the depths, to where his parents were gone, to beyond the spheres of this world or any other. His eyes began to flutter. He saw a bright white light that emanated from a source he could not see and felt himself slipping away.

What seemed like a few moments later, he opened his eyes.

Quiet. There was a clean smell to the air. He shifted uncomfortably. He was lying on some wooden boards. He was thirsty.

'Tom … Tommy boy!'

A face came into focus. Full lips, dark eyes. Someone was holding his hand. A head bent down towards him, dark-haired, silver earrings bobbing.

Zita.

His heart surged, and he sat upright, then instantly wished he hadn't.

A pain, keen and fierce, pierced his arm. He looked down.

There, glinting on his wrist, was a silver bracelet, pinching into the flesh of his forearm.

He wept.

They were in a room furnished like Jack's rooms. Only everything was oddly flat and dull. Above the fireplace was a painting of Mundham Farm, its colours muted and dark.

Kit was slumped into a corner, his arm draped over the stuffed crocodile, breathing softly. The silver-haired boy acknowledged Tom with a half-nod. 'Master has us all.'

'It's taken more of a toll on Kit than on me.' Zita brushed a frond of hair away from her eyes.

'We're in the glass box?'

Zita nodded.

'His power is on us now. These bracelets ...'

'Can he see us?' Through the glass he could see Jack's rooms in the farmhouse. The chair in front of the desk where he usually sat was empty.

'I'm not sure. It's not as if, my darling, we can do anything.'

'Is there a way out?'

Kit snorted. 'You try.'

'Oh, Tommy darling, who would have thought we would end up like this? Not even a gramophone to keep us cheerful.' Tears trembled in her eyes, but she wiped them away. 'Now then, that won't do, will it? That's not what Nanny used to say. Chin up, shoulders back. Go on, try the door.'

Zita helped Tom up, and he limped to the door, scratching at the bracelet all the while. It was unpleasant, like having a bite or a sting.

The door was wooden and on a latch. It opened easily.

But a force almost unbearably fierce pushed him backwards in to the room, and the door slammed shut of its own accord.

'Windows?'

'Look out.'

They were floating in a sea of mist. Below them he could see a wall reaching downwards, but not the ground. Above him there was also a flat expanse of what he assumed was stone.

'Where are we?'

'I don't know ... I have my suspicions. This is some place of Jack's devising, or else it's a different kind of realm altogether.'

Tom shrank back from the window and his reflection in it. He saw how haggard he looked in the cold light. Zita slunk to the wooden floorboards and sat next to Kit, stroking the boy's hair gently. Tom patted his pockets.

But the wooden flute that Tanenwod had given him was gone. Jack must have taken it from him before shutting him up.

'No hope.'

'Come here, Tommy boy.'

They clung together, the boy born five hundred years ago, the girl from the 1920s, and the twenty-first-century boy; all of them with nothing left in the world.

'It was fun while it lasted. What do you think they'll put on my grave?'

'If you ever get one.'

They split apart, but kept their hands almost touching. Zita sighed.

'There must be something we could do,' Tom said.

Once more, Kit grunted and moaned. He was in pain; the silver bracelet seemed to be hurting him more keenly.

Tom began to look around, picking up the objects and studying them. A carriage clock, not ticking. Two lamps, burning with strange, weak light. A paperknife with a pearl handle. A model of a boat. This gave Tom pause. It looked like the one his parents had drowned in. It resembled it down to the last detail. If he looked closely, he thought he could even see two figures in the cabin. He passed over it quickly.

The diary of Margaret Ravenswood. He picked the bound volume up and flicked through it avidly, but the pages were empty of writing.

He could almost sense Jack laughing in the far distance. Everything felt weightless and unreal.

Kit coughed, spluttered and sat upright. He looked so weak and spent, his eyes and hair dull. Tom rushed to his side and held him in his arms. He felt thin and light.

'Thomas…'

'Here.' Tom gave Kit a glug from a healing draught. When it had entered his blood, he began to look a little pinker.

'It be all a'cause of me,' Kit muttered.

'No, Kit, no, it's not…it's all of us, we're all in this.'

They stood huddled together by the table in the centre.

'Have you tried breaking the glass?'

In answer, Zita picked up the paperweight and slung it at the transparent wall. It bounced off, falling uselessly to the wooden planks.

'How long have I been in here?'

Zita shrugged. 'I have no idea.' She indicated the grandfather clock with a slight incline of her head and raised an eyebrow. The clock was not ticking. It did not even have any hands. 'I don't know if time has any meaning here at all. We might have been here for years. Or we might be kept here for a second of earth's time.'

Tom prowled around the room, twisting his fingers together. 'When Jack put the bracelet on you, you said you could take it off.'

'Nanny used to call that cheek. It was the only thing I could think of to say. I wanted to show him that he didn't control all of me.'

Kit coughed again.

'You've known him the longest, Kit. What are his weaknesses?'

'Jack hath no weakness.'

'Is he part Samdhya now?'

Kit shrugged.

Tom bent down and handled the paperweight. It was blue with white swirls in it. It reminded him of the sky. He wondered if he would ever see that again.

'Something Rohenga said. The Samdhya leader…'

'You spoke with him?' Kit looked perturbed.

'Yes, I saw him in the woods. I saw many of them. I met another too, called Tanenwod. She gave me a flute, but Jack must have taken it when he sent me here.'

'And tried they not to kill you?' Kit sounded surprised.

'I wasn't sure. They're like animals, but they're also like angels – or something else.'

Kit stiffened. 'You made friends with one of the Good People?'

'Is that what you call them?'

'My mother did call them that.'

'They said I had to release the Captive; otherwise things would break apart.'

'But the Samdhya…' broke in Zita. 'They will attack. They said they would. They'll kill him.'

'An' us,' added Kit.

'They won't attack. They can't. Rohenga said the threat was a way of trying to scare him so they could work out his weak points.'

Kit put his head between his hands. 'Us shall be slaves, for aye.'

Tom remembered his dreams and the endless squares, each one smaller than the last; and when you got to the last, there was nothing there.

When you broke everything apart, there was nothing.

When you looked into the darkness, there was nothing.

A weight of dread fell upon him, making his limbs like lead.

He looked at Zita, hugging her knees by the window; at Kit, exhausted, lying on his back. Even they were almost destroyed, and they knew Jack, had known Jack, for years, for longer than Tom had been alive.

His eyes fell upon the model of the boat that his parents had died on. He knew Jack had put it there to torture him.

At first he let the grief flow through him, making its way through every part of his body until he thought he was nothing but sadness.

That's why he put it there, thought Tom. *I won't give in to him. I won't.* Slowly, a nub of resistance began to form in him. He thought of his parents. Of love.

He heaved himself up, striking the table with his fist. Kit sat upright. Zita glanced at him from under heavy lids.

'We won't stay here and rot. Listen. Rohenga said something to me. He said Jack is breaking things apart.

What they do – the Samdhya – is hold everything together. He said Jack was an evil thing. I saw that evil. He … he killed my parents.'

Saying it made the tears cascade down his cheeks.

Kit looked away. Zita touched Tom's arm gently. 'Oh, darling one. I'm so sorry.'

Tom put his hand over hers.

'We're all trapped.' Tom went right up to the glass and put his forehead on it. It wasn't cool, but warm and buzzing with energy. He could see into Jack's rooms. There was no sign of Jack. 'He's planned everything. He wanted to kill me. He never wanted me to take over. So …' He turned back to face Kit and Zita. 'We have to do something he's not going to expect.'

'What's that, Tommy? What can we do here? You saw yourself, we can't get out.'

Filled with an odd kind of glee, Tom ran to the window and peered out into the mist.

Then he grabbed the latch.

Chapter 19

My daughter has vanished. There is no other word for it. Every day I pray to God. Every day he does not answer me.

> —From a letter by the Rev. Laurence
> Ravenswood to his Diocesan Bishop,
> November 1846. The letter was never sent.

Tom could scarcely believe what he had done. He'd thrust open the window. He felt elated.

'What are you doing?' Zita jumped up, clutching her hands together. Kit moved sluggishly towards the window to shut it.

The elation did not last long. Mist was pouring into the room now, thick and cold, unpleasantly surging over their skin and all but blinding them.

Kit's shouts were mingled, confusedly, with Zita's

'Find each other!' Tom shouted. His voice sounded muffled and damp. The mist was seeping into his lungs, clammy and uncomfortable, groping at him, its tendrils seeming to flick at him all over. 'Zita! Kit!'

He grabbed indiscriminately near him and felt first a sleeve and then a hand. Its fingers closed onto his tightly.

'Thomas.' It was Kit. Kit linked his arm into Tom's. The welcome pressure of another body. The silver hair, dimly discerned.

'Zita!' Tom called.

'Here,' came a voice, seemingly far distant, and then suddenly her face was close to his, and those familiar dark eyes were blinking at him. Relief. He grasped her hand too, joining his own arm to hers.

'Stay together.'

'What if something comes in?'

A gust of wind blew into the room, making them huddle together. The cold was almost unbearable. There was a howl, like a wolf, and then the beating of wings. They braced themselves.

And then the mist began to clear, and within a few seconds they could make out each other's features.

They stood, panting, regarding each other in the strange light. Beyond the glass of their prison, Jack's rooms remained as they had always been; they had never felt so far away.

'You might have killed us, Tommy boy.' Zita drew him to her, hardly able to disguise her relief, and pulled Kit into the embrace too.

After a second or two, they released each other. Kit was wide-eyed. 'He maun come.'

'He's not here yet,' said Zita.

'At least now we know we can open the window. He wouldn't have expected that. Keep together. Let's go.' Tom spoke decisively, though he was trembling.

They reached the window, and Tom, letting go of the others' hands, peered out gingerly. A freezing blast of wind blew the hair into his eyes. He pushed it away.

'What dost see?' It was Kit, awe in his voice. Something was changing within him; some realisation was coming to the fore, that he was disobeying Jack for the first time in several hundred years. It seemed to both exhaust and exhilarate him at once.

Tom looked down. 'Something that looks like the ground.'

'How far away is it?' This was Zita, crowding to the sill.

'I don't know. It's hard to tell.'

'We maun die there.' Kit was suddenly deflated, his voice hollow.

'It's better than being in here. We'll probably die in here too.'

The cold meant that Tom could hardly feel his fingers. He blew on them. 'There's nothing to hold onto. The wall looks smooth. You couldn't get a grip on it.'

'How about jumping?'

'I can't tell what's down there.'

Zita felt around her neck. The locket with John Temple's obituary in it.

'Don't!'

'It's the only thing we have.'

'Wait!' Tom took out a vial which held a healing draught.

He unstoppered it and offered it to Kit and Zita. They shared it, welcoming the tang of herbs. Zita let the locket fall gently back onto her throat, and then Kit leant over the windowsill and dropped the vial.

They all listened and shortly heard a soft thud as it landed.

'There must be something there. Something we can walk on. Something that will lead us away.'

Tom was filled with new purpose. He kept glancing to the door, the real door, in Jack's chambers. But still the room was undisturbed. Where was Jack? What was he doing? Was he waiting somewhere, toying with them? They had to move quickly.

'It's so dark out there.' Zita bit her lip.

'Lights!' It was Kit who spoke, and Tom saw an intensity burning in his eyes he'd never seen before.

They searched around the room, knowing that at any second Jack might return and discover what they were doing.

The two dim lamps on the mantelpiece were the only sources of light. They glowed without real flame and, when Tom passed a finger through the top of one of them, did not even give off heat.

Then they faced the window. Outside, the blackness seemed thick, unbearable. It was like being in the belly of some terrible beast or in the deepest coalmine. The shadows lay thickly on top of each other. It was as if no ray of light had ever penetrated it.

Just as Tom was steeling himself to take the first jump, Zita said, 'I can send myself.'

'No, Zita, you can't do it. You'll be in too much pain.'

'Bottoms up,' she said. And before anybody could do anything to stop her, Zita closed her eyes and started to mutter under her breath. It appeared as if she was going into a trance. Her eyes fluttered under her eyelids; she shuddered, and then went limp.

Kit immediately put his arms around her. 'Gone.'

'How long will she be away?'

'Time be not the same.'

Tom remembered the bells striking in White Quad. The boy, standing there, unsure, in his ill-fitting uniform. The smell of cut grass on the breeze. The summer sun filtering through the plane tree and the shadows on the lawn. What wouldn't he give to hear the comforting ringing now, or even the nasal voice of Fletcher, calling him to supper, the bleep of computer games, the gush of a tap running.

Tom peered out again into the darkness. It did not seem any less impenetrable. He placed one of the lamps on the windowsill. It was laughably weak.

Kit regarded him with both longing and fear. Tom held him, and they hugged each other, waiting, Zita between them.

After a few seconds, a spluttering came from Zita, and she sat upright, eyes open. She looked even paler than before, a bluish, unhealthy tinge to her skin.

She spoke hesitantly. 'I've seen what's out there, chaps.'

'We can get out?' Tom let go of Kit, and Kit, in turn, released Zita.

Zita nodded. 'I think so.'

Kit said, ''Tis a dread sight.'

'Can you send yourself out of here? Out of this ... place?'

Zita shook her head. 'I've already tried. I reach a wall I can't get through. A wall made by Jack ... so we are in some place made by him. Some place that uses the house as a pattern.'

Tom leaned out further.

'Tom, there's something out there. And this wall is all around it. But there's something else. A deeper darkness. If we can reach that, then we will be able to find the way out.'

'Like a disc? Like a black disc?'

Zita looked puzzled.

'A flat, round thing?' he said.

'A bit like that ... why?'

'I saw something like that ... When I found the place where the Captive was held. Jack sent me to the day when my parents died. And I saw this black circle hovering above me. I managed to get to it, and it sent me back to him.'

'Do you think it might lead to him?'

'I don't know. He might be expecting it; he might not be.'

'Then are we ready?'

'I am loath to ...' Kit suddenly said. 'I seen enough. I been enough with him. I shall stay here, an' he will do what he will wi' me.'

'Kit, you mustn't!' Zita, despite her pain, scrambled towards him.

'I shall not do it ...'

'Why not? It's not Jack, is it?'

Kit sobbed. It was a shock, in the stillness of the space, to hear him cry. Zita immediately grasped his hands, but he pushed her off. Tom stood warily near.

'Shall kill me …'

'Who?'

'Her.' Kit swallowed, and his Adam's apple stood out in his throat.

A light dawned in Tom's mind. 'The … black space, the disc. What's in there? What do you think's in there?'

Zita looked alarmed.

'I … I done it,' sobbed Kit once more. 'I made it.'

'Did what?' Tom remembered the tenderness with which Jack, hundreds of years ago, had stroked Kit's hair. 'Made what?'

Kit controlled himself. 'He could not take one of the Good Folk on his own. How could he? And she sware revenge.'

'Who did? Who did, Kit?'

With a great wrench, Kit raised himself up. He was trembling. 'I done it. I took the Captive. And the Captive hath sworn vengeance on me; an' she find me, she shall slay me.' He gripped the sides of his head with his hands.

'I thought so!' Zita gasped. 'I felt it in the darkness. There's something there, kept there, all tied up.'

'So he's put us in here to be killed by him or by the Captive,' said Tom. 'All of us.'

Death if they stayed; death if they left.

Suddenly, he half-dragged Kit to the windowsill and, ignoring his cries of protest and Zita's warnings, scrambled onto the ledge, holding Kit tightly, grabbed the lamp resting there and, taking a deep breath, leapt into the blackness.

As he fell, Tom had no time to think about what they might meet on the ground.

In the end, it was almost instantaneous. One minute he was falling; the next he was sprawled on soft earth. He'd landed with Kit, and the two of them had rolled over for a second or two, before coming to a standstill.

Half a second later, there was a thud beside them, and the glow of a dim lamp.

'Well, luckily I was always rather good at that sort of thing,' came Zita's voice, and Tom was glad to hear it. 'Escaping out of the dorm and all that.'

'Anyone hurt?'

'I don't think so,' said Tom. Kit merely groaned.

'We'll have to drag him,' said Zita. 'We can manage him between us.'

Behind them was the outline of a sheer stone building, and they could just see a space where the window had been.

The cold was now biting. Huddled together, they kept Kit in between the two of them. Tom's right side was almost numb. They held the lamps in their outer hands. The rays did not help much, but they moved in a small circle of orange that was almost cheerful compared to the blackness outside it.

'How do we know which direction to go in?'

'I'll have to send myself.'

'Zita! You can't.'

In the odd light, her face was set into an expression that Tom recognised. It showed the will that had taken her into the farm, the will that had made her disobey her parents. 'You can't stop me.'

And so they went onwards. Zita would close her eyes and go limp, and send herself a few hundred feet ahead, trying to conserve as much of her energy as she could.

Whilst she was gone, Tom would stand, supporting both his friends, enveloped by blackness, staring only at the light from his tiny lamp. He tried to keep his mind focused on the flame, and ignore the emptiness surrounding him.

It was so much worse than being on the boat. He wondered if death was like this, and his mind kept edging towards despair.

Zita would then return. Each time she was noticeably weaker. The fourth time she did it, it took her a long time to get back to normal, during which Tom began to think that they all might turn to ice. He had no idea how much time was passing. It seemed sometimes to be hours.

'You've got to help me, Kit,' he said. 'Please.'

But Kit did not respond.

When she next returned, she could barely walk. 'It's not far off,' she said and then stumbled and fell.

Tom grabbed her. 'Come on, Zita, you can do it.'

Kit sat down on the ground.

'I can't do this on my own! Please, Kit, please!'

There was a rumbling sound, coming from somewhere far away.

'I think,' whispered Zita, 'that means he's noticed.'

Tom put Zita's arm over his shoulder and grabbed Kit by the arm. The boy got up sluggishly.

'I will face the Captive. Rather her than him again.'

Tom squeezed his arm in thanks.

The three of them half-ran, half-stumbled, in a straight line, through the cold, the rumbling behind them growing, now seeming like a human roar of rage.

There was a burst of light behind them, illuminating the nothingness, showing a great wide plain.

Near in front of them was the darker blackness, the anomaly that Zita had noted.

'Jack's in the house. The... thing... it's just ahead...' slurred Zita. She could hardly move. 'Go, Tommy, go. Leave me here. I'll do it one more time. It will stop him for a bit.' She was wilting, her knees bent. Tom grabbed her, though he was fading too.

His whole body felt weak, as if he'd been climbing a mountain. The air was thin. Every gulp of breath cost him. He faltered.

The light focused into a beam and started to track across the wasteland. Zita shook and went limp.

The light behind them paused. Tom and Kit pushed themselves onwards, dragging Zita between them.

A sudden spasm shook the girl, and Zita came spluttering back. 'He saw me. He's furious.' She was shaking with cold and fear.

'Where is it, Zita, where is it?'

'Only a few steps further.'

They fell to the ground now, all three of them, and crawled. It was hard. What was under their fingers was cold, earth-like, unyielding. They stayed as close to each other as they could.

The beam, tracking from side to side, was getting nearer. As it lit up a strip behind them, they saw, directly in front of it, a mere hand's-breadth away, a darkness greater than all around it.

'All at the same time,' breathed Tom.

They reached forwards, just as the beam focused on them and grew stronger and the roar of Jack's rage reached a terrifying pitch. They touched the darkness, and something gave way, and there was a pitching and a lurching as they were heaved about, and then there was nothing but silence, a light and a pair of eyes, glinting.

Chapter 20

Trap us, and we are yet free.

—From the Sayings of the Samdhya,
transcribed by Margaret Ravenswood

A warm golden light came from some source Tom could not see. They were in a large square room with no windows, decorated with tapestries, a comfortable-looking bed to one side, draped in rich clothes. A loom stood near it. There was no door.

His heart quailed. They had escaped from one prison only to arrive in another. Zita stumbled and was sick, retching violently, and stood for a moment with her head resting against the wall. Kit was at least upright.

But he was staring at something, his body trembling, his mouth gaping, an unmistakeable look of terror in his eyes. Tom could see a whiteness reflected in them, like the flicker of a ghost. He turned round.

In the centre of the room, iron chains on her wrists and manacles on her legs, with long dark hair streaked with white and a leopard tattoo on her right cheek, dressed in a long, simple white robe, was a tall, willowy Samdhya. She was gaunt, and dark hollows were under her eyes. She was shivering.

She looked up slowly, taking in the three of them, drinking in their faces.

She paid particular attention to Kit. A cruel smile spread over her face.

'You … the one who took me … you have come to mock me in my captivity?' She laughed gutturally. Her accent was the same as Rohenga's, slightly foreign with the syllables sometimes stressed in the wrong places. 'For only the one who captured me can release me. Why else would you come? Surely not to pass the time of day.'

Kit whimpered.

'No, it's not like that.' Tom tried to think. 'We've come to set you free.'

The Captive examined her nails and showed her long teeth. 'A brave crew the three of you are. I do not know how much time has passed since I have been here. It may have been many centuries of your time. I occupy myself with making things. He cannot prevent me from doing that. My will is strong still, for some things. You saw some of them, did you not? He keeps them. He learns from them.' She turned her gaze onto Tom and the fierceness in it made him quiver.

'And you, Zita, the girl who can send herself. It is not often that we see a talent like that. And he keeps you all to himself.'

'We haven't got much time – he's right behind us.' Zita's voice was shaky.

'Know that I will kill that one,' spat the Captive, raising her wrist with difficulty and pointing at Kit. 'I will kill him the moment I am released. And then after I have done with him, I will have my revenge on James Swinton, and on his spawn too, and on those who have executed his will.'

The Captive held her chains out. 'Shall you free me now?'

'He's coming,' gasped Zita. The walls of the room shook, as if hit by a small earthquake.

'One of the peculiarities of my imprisonment. I can hold him off, for a while at least.'

'There must be another way. If we free you, won't you forgive Kit? It wasn't his fault.'

'What do you have to say for yourself, Christopher?' The Captive smiled, but it was the smile of a wolf. Tom noticed that there were marks around her wrists from where the manacles touched her skin.

A moan came from where Kit was standing, holding his head with both his hands.

'A terrible choice. Free me and be killed. Or wait until Jack breaks through and be killed too.'

'Shall bargain wi' thee.' It was Kit, his voice weak.

'Don't. She'll twist it somehow!' Zita spoke louder.

'She will not.' Kit neared the Captive. 'She will not a'cause I took her. This be my bargain. I set thee free, and thou shalt kill me. Spare them. They need Jack dead. Even more'n I do.'

Kit placed his hands on the iron manacles around the Captive's wrists. The room shook especially hard, as if Jack could sense what was happening. Kit muttered a few words and sobbed.

It was over in a second.

The chains were off.

Almost immediately the Captive snapped the irons around her legs. She stretched and yawned, stood for a second surveying the room. Tom had the sensation that here was something like a bolt of lightning or a hawk.

And then, with a movement fast and precise, she picked Kit up by the throat.

Tom ran at her and tried to prise her fingers away. Kit was choking, the veins bulging underneath his skin, his eyelids fluttering, his eyeballs rolling back into his skull. He was dangling a foot off the ground, clutching at the Samdhya's arms, his legs kicking in the air.

But it was already too late.

Kit was choking. The Samdhya was too strong and growing stronger. She now took up more space, looking more like Rohenga than she had done before, those eyes, dark and animal and yet so beguiling at the same time.

Tom wished once more for the flute. If only he could call Tanenwod to help them.

With a final effort, Kit wheezed, struggled and then went still.

'He's dead.' Zita sobbed.

The Captive released him, letting him drop as if he were

223

nothing, and sighed with satisfaction. 'So easy to harm you mortals. We protect you, and yet really you are nothing.'

Tom watched Kit slump onto his front, lying askew. His hair hung limply over his face, hiding his eyes. He looked like a broken doll.

Tom felt so helpless. Zita let out a low moan. They clung to each other.

'And now …' The Captive, lordly and disdainful, her white robe rustling, her eyes glowing, turned towards where Tom and Zita huddled together.

She regarded them for a second or two, as if deciding what to do with them. Tom started forwards but Zita held him back.

At that moment, the walls of the room shook and shivered and burst open, and there, standing in a blaze of light, dressed in a long black tailcoat, was Tom's enemy, his uncle, his ancestor, the slayer of his parents. Jack Swinton.

The landscape around them was illuminated, the mist blew away and they could see, in the near distance, a black building which must have been where they had been kept, the dark shadow of the farmhouse existing in a separate plane of reality.

Jack came striding along, coat tails billowing and swirling out behind him, a nightmare of anger, fists clenched and face grim.

He faced up to the Captive. The pair of them looked equal to each other, Jack tall and strong. They circled each other for a moment. Then Jack bowed. The Captive merely raised an eyebrow in return, and Jack, pausing for a second to acknowledge the gesture, went straight to Kit.

His demeanour changed, softened. He relaxed a little, bending down so that he could be near the boy, whose dull silver hair was spread out beneath him.

'My boy, my sweet boy.' He sank down, placed his hands on the boy's heart, and Kit shuddered with life. 'He lives yet.'

As if satisfied, he stood, turned, his gaze lingering on Zita for an uncomfortable second, and then addressed Tom. He curled his lip and almost spat out the words: 'I thought you were a true Swinton. It seems I was wrong.'

Tom bristled. 'You wanted to kill me! That's why you brought me here. Not to keep me and train me up, but because I'm the only one who can kill you!'

Jack smiled. 'Clever. Clever indeed. But you cannot stop me, Thomas.'

The Samdhya laughed. The two of them were squaring up to each other now. 'You are the breaker of things, James Swinton. This has continued too long. You must have noticed, as you wandered in places not meant for you. You have lived beyond the normal order. It is only for the Samdhya to live like this. It is time for you to end.'

'And I kept you here for long. You were not powerful enough to stand against me.'

'You had the help of Christopher. The one who had the power. You could not have done it without him.'

'It is true. That is why I kept him with me all those years.'

'I didn't want to do it. You made me.' Kit sobbed. He looked so weak, so young.

'Kit, Kit, Kit. That isn't true, is it? You loved it just as much as I did. You loved the power.'

The old man knelt, stroked Kit's cheek and cradled him, as if he were a father holding a wounded son.

Kit sobbed, his whole body tensing. As Jack drew a strand of hair away from his face, Tom saw that attached to a string around Jack's neck was a wooden flute.

It was the one Tanenwod had given him.

If only he could get to it!

Jack looked up, as if sensing the direction Tom was looking in. 'You may think you've freed her. But she cannot get over the moat. She can only kill us. And that she will not be able to do. Kit will stand with me against her, will you not, my boy?'

In answer, Kit simply shook with sobs.

'I won't,' said Zita. 'I won't fight the Captive.'

'Then you'll die.'

'I don't think so,' said Tom. 'She needs one of us to take her over the moat. She'll keep one of us alive.'

'Then let it be you, Tom.' Zita's voice was dull. 'I've lived too long. I have nothing left.'

'We'll live,' said Tom. 'All of us. I promise you, Zita.' He took her hand and squeezed her fingers. The pressure was returned. A look of determination had come into her eyes, a look that he now knew well. If he could only get through this and be with Zita, it would be all right.

'So is this to be the final battle?' mocked the Samdhya. 'Is this how we array our forces? On a wasted plain. On one side, I, a Swinton and one of your slaves. On the other, James Swinton, who has kept me captured so long, and your boy, whom I have already all but killed?'

'It doesn't have to be like this,' said Tom. Before he knew what he was doing, he launched himself at Jack, and with a sudden movement tore the flute from his neck. The chain snapped, and then he was holding it, feeling its warmth beneath his fingers, the breath of Tanenwod. He saw Jack's look of surprise and the Captive's quizzical expression.

Springing forwards, Jack wrested the flute back from Tom.

They fought. Tom hung off Jack's wrist, trying to force open his grip. The old man was strong and savage and managed to fling him away, only for Zita to run at him and knock the flute out of his hand.

It dropped onto the ground and rolled away. Tom was on it in a second.

The note that came out was surprisingly rich and deep.

There was silence. The little group stood in a circle, in the darkness, lit only by the pale flames of the lamps, Tom in the centre, Jack by himself, chest puffed out and head raised high, Zita, crouched in a defensive position, near the Captive, who stood with one knee bent, a slight grin on her face, and Kit lying on his side, white and downcast.

There was a sound like the bird scarers Tom had heard when he'd first arrived at Mundham Farm. The ground shook.

Jack said, 'What have you done?' He sounded hoarse, perplexed. 'What have you done? What spell is this? I do not know it. I do not know it! It's …' Tom blew the flute again and the note swelled. Jack shuddered, and the bird scarers grew louder, and they were drums, beating loud and wild.

'Your powers give way, James Swinton. You see. Now.'

'I don't understand. My wards are breaking. This world is breaking apart.'

There was a terrible scream from James, as if he were being run through with a sword, and the world swung from side to side. Everything lurched and Tom was reminded of the sickening movement of the boat during the storm that killed his parents, and then everything righted again.

Immediately Tom could smell the fresh Suffolk air. He almost dropped to the ground right there and kissed the grass. He was even grateful to hear the sound, somewhere in the near distance, of a motor.

They were standing on the island, in daylight, the farmhouse in its warm red brick behind them, the spire of the church beyond, and above them the clouds were gathering, and the Captive started to sing, and somehow Tom knew what she was singing.

She was singing that the Wildmark were riding, that the Storm was coming, that the Deep were here. From out of a black cloud swooped a hawk, and then another, plunging like an arrow to the bridge, and the Captive held her arms out and greeted them with joy. A thunderclap rumbled and lightning forked through the grey skies. The wind was rising.

The trees shivered, and from between the trunks came surging a host of animals, deer and foxes and badgers, stoats and weasels and otters and what must have been a wolf, and then for a second they were not animals, but beautiful, tall people on white and black horses, galloping towards the island.

Within a second they were surrounded. Everywhere you looked there was a mounted Samdhya, everywhere the sound of a horse snorting. Some of them looked as if they were half animal, had still retained some aspect of their animal self in a badger's snout or a raven's wings.

A hare leapt forwards. It turned and turned in the air, seeming to dance, and then, in its place, armed with a sword and a spear, a quiver on her back, dressed in dark greens and browns, was Tanenwod.

'Light on the Water.' She did not bow, but it was clear from her bearing that she was in awe of the Captive.

'And now,' said the Captive. 'James Swinton has been warping the world for too long. It is time to set things right.'

Tanenwod threw a dagger over the water, and the Captive caught it with one hand and offered it to Tom.

It was silver, studded with jewels, curved and engraved with ornate symbols that Tom understood in the same way that he had understood the tapestries the Samdhya had made. Truth was there, the wonderful, coruscating truth of the universe, and he knew that if he killed Jack it would be known to him. It was a glimpse of light, of the space between things, as true as the curve of a raven's beak, as the point of a wolf's tooth, as the bite in the winter wind.

Kit was holding his hands over his ears, but there was hope in his eyes. Zita was next to him, one hand on Kit's shoulder, the other curled into a fist.

Tom knew now why Tanenwod had chosen to live with the Samdhya. The beat of the Samdhya's drums was entering into Tom's blood.

In Jack he saw centuries of darkness. He saw a twisted, terrible thing, that could have been bright and pure, that had corrupted, stewed, degraded.

He stood, trembling, with the dagger raised, poised. It was heavy in his hand.

In the lines of James's face, he saw his own father's features.

And he also saw his own, as in a mirror.

And when James opened his mouth and spoke, he spoke in Tom's own voice.

'Please. Don't. Don't kill me.'

The clouds above Tom, swirling and dark. The crowd of Samdhya, their animal noises and faces, their terrible strength and beauty.

He stood there, his whole arm shaking, the tip of the knife a foot away from James. It sang to him. There was only one possible direction it could go in, one answer to the torturous question, one simple solution.

'You have forgotten something,' said James quietly.

As at a command, the bracelet on Tom's wrist began to cut deeply into his flesh. He almost dropped the knife.

'I have power still. It can pierce your veins in a second. What an impasse we are at.'

The pain was deep, reaching his bones. He tightened his grip. Zita and Kit were also clutching at their wrists, red streams of blood flowing down their forearms.

'Is this how it finishes, James Swinton? You, alone, facing me?' The Captive was mocking still. The sense of intention from the watching Samdhya was hard to bear.

Tom was giving way. His vision was blurring. The knife was wavering. He would drop it. He would drop it and be killed, and would die on the soil of the house his ancestor had built. The house that should have been his father's, that should have been his. And Kit would die too, and Zita, at last, as they should have done, and everything would be righted again.

Struggling, he faltered.

He closed his eyes. Everything seemed impossibly far away. He was getting cold. There was a sound like the surge of waves.

He thought of the sea. A different time, when he had sat by the shoreline, his mother encouraging him to paddle, the brightness of the sun so enticing, his father scooping him up when he fell.

Something warm touched his hand. He opened his eyes groggily.

Leana, her soft, pink, warm tongue caressing his fingers. Leana, her bright black eyes looking at him quizzically, ears pricked, body lithe and tense.

Leana. The normality of her brought him back to the moment. James, standing tall on the lawn. The Captive, poised to kill. Kit and Zita, nearly on their knees with pain from their bracelets. Beyond the moat, the rustling of spears and horses. The flash of a scarlet tattoo on a cheek.

And Tom started to think. Why did James ask him here? He was the only one who could kill him. That would mean he must have the same kinds of power as James. He'd said his father had had none, or James would have brought him closer too. Perhaps he had more than anyone in his family since James.

Tom had been making the wards. He had been able to manipulate the illusions on the boat. He had fought and beaten the younger version of Jack.

Keeping his eyes closed, he focused on the bracelet on his wrist. He tested its boundaries. It was alive with dark energy. He could feel it searing into him.

He searched around tentatively, for a kink, for a knot, for a gap.

Ignoring a sudden burst of pain, he continued to test it, gently feeling along it.

The pain was tearing deep into him.

Concentrating hard, he willed himself not to lose control. *Come on*, he thought. *Come on, there must be something*.

And then he found it. A tiny knot in the make-up of the spell. He could feel it.

It was Kit. Something there that he could push at. A space where he could reach in and unpick. He sent in a tendril of his own power. It was weaker. He tested it, carefully, subtly. James was still focused on Kit and Zita and on keeping apart from the Captive. All around him hung in tension.

And, slowly, Tom began to take the spell apart.

James did not notice at first. Kit was unconscious now, and Zita was almost there.

There it was. He sent out a burst of his own energy into the spell that made the bracelet and felt it dissolve.

And now the bracelet gave way. With a slow gesture, he pulled at it and tugged it off, brandishing it. James snapped his attention towards him. Those lizard eyes were on him.

And Tom threw the bracelet towards the moat. It arced, and sent back a glimmer of light, before falling into the water.

Jack hesitated. Tom held his breath.

Then everything happened very quickly. Without really thinking what he was doing, Tom raced to the Captive and lifted her up over his shoulder. She was surprisingly light. Leana started barking madly and danced between Tom and Jack.

Tom ran towards the bridge.

The gate was closed.

A ray of light began to pierce through the clouds.

The latch was on. He fumbled with it. A shout came from Jack, hoarse and panicked.

Don't look back now.

He forced the gate open and stepped onto the bridge.

Almost immediately the Captive cried out in pain.

'Run!' she cried, her voice sounding almost like the squawk of a bird. 'Run, quickly, or I shall die!' She began to feel heavier.

The bridge was only ten feet long. The Captive was screaming, her weight growing more difficult to bear by the second.

At the other end of the bridge loomed the massed ranks of the Samdhya, and as Tom ran, each step harder and harder, they seemed to merge into each other, becoming a many-headed beast.

The gate at the other end was closed too, but as he reached it, Tanenwod stepped forwards from out of the throng and opened it, standing back to let him pass.

A burst of rage came from Jack. Tom dropped the Captive down onto the grass and was about to collapse next to her, just as a ball of furious energy came crashing into his back, knocking him flat onto his face, and then all he saw was whiteness, and all he heard was his name, in his father's voice, being called over and over again, and the patter of rain.

The wind was howling now. Tom struggled to his feet, rain streaking across his face. The Captive whooped a war cry, and the Samdhya danced around her, beating their drums, some turning into birds and swooping around her, others racing round and round.

Three figures remained on the island. Zita, now comforting Kit, and Jack, whose face was stricken with anger. They were all drenched, their clothes streaming, and the sky once more shook with thunder, electricity humming in the air.

For a moment Tom thought Jack might give in.

'Kit,' said Jack. 'My boy...'

'No!' screamed Kit. And he ran at him, tearing at Jack, beating at him with his fists.

Jack was too strong for Kit. He was going to kill him, as the rain poured down around them, forming into puddles at their feet, bouncing off the moat, flattening their hair to their skulls.

Tom knew now that this was his fight. He was the only one who could kill Jack.

He felt a tug at his arm. It was Tanenwod. He understood her look. He nodded at her and, taking a deep breath, he ran back across the moat, holding the dagger. Zita tried to stop him, but he shrugged her off.

'Jack,' said Tom, confronting him, 'this dagger has been made for you.'

'You can't do it,' sneered Jack, throwing Kit to one side. 'You are too soft. I have power still!' He squeezed his hand into a fist, and Tom felt a terrible tightness around his neck. He fought blindly against it. It faded.

Jack looked surprised and readied himself for another attack. But he was panting now, and he looked old, stooping, bowed, the weight of the centuries and his wickedness pressing down upon him.

'That you may,' answered Tom. The lightning struck once more and Jack's whole face was lit with devilish brightness, and the crowd of Samdhya beyond the moat seemed at once animal and human, a chaos of feather and tooth and horn. 'But so do I.'

Sensing the energy around him, Tom, with a surge of power, lashed out towards Jack, wrapping him in thick tendrils of smoke, chaining him about with wards until all that could be seen were Jack's eyes, and all that could be heard was a muffled roar.

'You're right, Jack. I can't kill you. I am too soft. I know you killed my parents. I know I should kill you. But I can't.'

'What will you do, then, Thomas Swinton?' Jack was dissolving the wards, his face clear now, his grin apparent.

Tom smiled. He lifted a hand. A window shattered above them, and out of the house came, at Tom's command, the glass box.

He made it hover in between them, so that Jack was reflected back to himself, and so that Jack could see Tom's face through it. The thunder was rolling so deeply, and caught up in the drums and whoops of the Samdhya, all now whirling around the island, the trees stretching their branches, crows and jackdaws and rooks flapping all around, and Tom yelled from the depths of his stomach.

A second later, Jack was not there any more. He was inside the box. Tom could see Jack's teeth, bared in a grin.

Without any more thought, Tom hurled the box down onto the bridge; and it smashed into thousands of glittering pieces.

There was a silence. Water flowing through the moat. The farmhouse seemed to shiver for a second or two, as if, having been held up by Jack all these years, it might collapse. Then it settled. On the island, Kit and Zita were clutching each other. Zita's eye make-up had run, and Kit's hair was flattened to his face. Leana had vanished. The Samdhya seemed, on the other side of the bridge, to be absolutely still, rank upon rank of tall, long-haired warriors, tattoos bright on their cheeks, some with horns sprouting from their foreheads, and one even with wings from her back. The Captive was standing before them all, and she glowed, bright, like a star.

Tom collapsed onto his knees, rain pouring down his cheeks and into his clothes, and sank his head onto the sodden grass.

A hawk settled on the bridge, gripping the rail with its claws. Zita yelled something Tom could not quite hear. There was a barking, a hooting.

And the Samdhya, loud and strong, like meltwater rushing into the river, exploded into cries of triumph.

Chapter 21

I went to the monument we built for her, outside the church walls. A simple thing, a stone, and her name. Someone had placed a rose upon it, although it was December. I saw a wild figure standing by the church door, and I thought it was my daughter. And then the figure was gone; a hare scudded by me, and the sun pooled on the stone, and the scent of the petals filled me with joy.

—From the papers of the Rev. Laurence
Ravenswood, dated 1875

The sun was low in the sky and the air was still and clear. It was towards evening, on the day that Tom had trapped Jack in the glass and smashed it. Moving slowly across the lawn in front of Mundham Farm, beyond the bridge, was a group of four people, a black lurcher weaving in between them.

At first glance, they seemed like any other group of young friends. Looking closer, you would see that one of them, a willowy girl with long black hair and an unearthly gleam in her eyes, was carrying a short sword in a sheath around her waist. The girl with whom she was walking arm in arm, sported an old-fashioned haircut as if she was on her way to a 1920s themed ball. She was twirling a string of pearls around her neck and smiling as she spoke.

Behind them, walking slightly apart, were two teenaged boys. One, with his blond hair shaggier than it had ever been, was limping slightly, dressed in a pair of jeans and a white T-shirt. The other was all in black. But what was even more striking about him was his hair, which was black as a raven's feather, and his eyes, which were blue and animated, though he looked tired and pale and as if he hadn't eaten in a long time. Sometimes he leaned on his companion and they halted frequently, as he clutched at his chest in apparent pain.

In the near distance, on the mound, a shadowy figure stood, watching and listening, raising its hand as if to show that all was well.

Zita paused, letting her pearls rest against her neck, and removed her arm from Tanenwod's. 'The sun's setting.' She turned to the Samdhya, puckering her forehead. 'Why didn't you tell me? I was waiting for you. I knew you were here, I knew it. Maybe that's partly why I found my way here, all those years ago.'

'Zita Ravenswood. My brother's grand-daughter. My great-niece. I never knew you. But I saw you. And I see my brother in you.' Tanenwod smiled tenderly.

'He never talked about you. I suppose people didn't talk about things they didn't understand. Do they still do that, Tommy boy?'

Behind them, Tom shrugged.

Margaret Ravenswood, whose name amongst the Samdhya was Tanenwod, reached out to stroke the line of Zita's cheek and for a moment held her hand there. Then she sighed. 'I must return to the Wildmark. Tonight we must begin repairing what James has wrought. It will be a long, hard task.'

She gazed across into the woods. As Zita turned away, Tanenwod caught her by the wrist. 'Zita, you could come with me. You could become like us. There is so much we see, so much we do. You have looked into my eyes. You need only look for a little longer and you will change,'

Zita glanced back at Tom and Kit, who were throwing sticks to Leana. The lurcher was catching them and zooming about in lunatic circles. 'I have work to do here.'

Tanenwod released her. 'I understand. Your fellows. Kit, he will need help. And Thomas Swinton ...' She didn't finish her thought, though the silence hung heavily between them. 'But when you need me, you have the flute. And we will be watching, always.'

She kissed Zita. Tom ran to her, and then, uncertain whether to hug her or not, simply bowed. Kit remained further away and just touched his fingers to his forehead.

Tanenwod returned the bow, became a hare and bounded away, and the three were left together, the house's solid red brick behind them, and they stood in a circle, holding hands. Tom looked at each of them and could not decide which one he loved the most.

There were things to do. There were dinners to make and clear away. The horse needed to be fed and exercised. But they no longer had to do the bounds.

Kit was exhausted. He could not, or would not, go very far from the house, and Tom helped him back and, having made some hot tinned tomato soup for him, discovered for the first time where he slept, in a small white-washed room with a single bed tucked up next to the library, a single book on the bedside table. It was a prayerbook, ancient, its pages browning. Kit went for it and held it, muttering under his breath.

'He's gone, Kit, he's gone!' Tom said.

The boy, though, was shattered, and when Tom closed the door, Kit cried out as in a nightmare. Leana crept up the stairs and sat protectively in front of the room.

'Give him time,' said Zita when Tom came to her. She too was drifting from room to room, opening windows into the gathering dusk, lighting candles and setting flowers in vases. The gramophone was on, playing a gentle trumpet tune. 'He was with Jack for longer than any of us. All those hundreds of years as Jack's bondsman...' She let the sentence drift away.

She was right. And Tom found himself rushing around the house, as if he might find some avatar of Jack hidden away. He turned on all the electric lights. Zita had placed flowers in every room. There were no hidden spaces, no extra rooms, no sense of bending time and space.

Gingerly, he entered the attic and found there only one large empty room with an initialled trunk in one corner, cobwebs and dust everywhere. The seven doors, the wraiths and all trace of Jack Swinton, it seemed, had vanished.

Kit appeared an hour or so later, when they were cooking dinner, Leana at his heels. Tom and Zita had opened tin after tin of tuna and sardines and olives and were boiling pasta. He stood and hovered in the doorway. Zita was wearing a black sparkly dress and had woven a feather into her hair. Her eyes were still shadowed. Tom himself was immensely hungry, and his jeans hung loosely on his waist.

Kit looked rested. But he also seemed troubled.

'What's the matter, Kit-Kat?' Zita twirled.

'I don't need your larks now, Zita.'

'Oh, don't be such a spoilsport.' She kissed him on the cheek.

Kit scowled. Then he suddenly grabbed a bunch of flowers from the china vase and stormed out. Looking askance at Tom, Zita followed him, and Tom came behind.

Kit led them up to the study.

'He's gone,' said Zita, as they stood on the threshold. At first none of them wanted to step inside. A faint uneasiness hung about, as if somehow Jack might still be lurking in a hidden recess, a shadow, a gap in reality that they were not aware of, could not be aware of.

'I can't believe it, quite.'

They went in. Tom turned on the light and the room seemed to have lost something. The floorboards creaked under their feet. The stuffed crocodile's eyes were dull, its skin dusty. The vials were empty. There was Jack's desk, no longer forbidding and strange. The desk drawer came open when Tom tried it, and inside it was the box. It was a lovely thing, carved and jewelled.

'Don't touch it.'

Tom sensed around it with his mind. 'It's all right. There's nothing in it.' He placed his hand on it. It held no power now.

Kit nodded and picked it up. Then he stalked out, and the others, slightly at a loss, followed him. He grabbed a torch from the kitchen. The moon was bright and the evening was warm. Behind them the farmhouse was lit up, lights in every room.

They followed him over the dark lawn to the woods. Kit walked with determination, not answering Tom or Zita's questions as they trotted to keep up with him, until they reached a clearing.

'Here,' he said, switching off the torch. ''Twas here.'

He laid the box down in the moonlight on the forest floor, and the flowers beside it, and removed the prayerbook from his pocket, and knelt on the earth. The trees around them rustled and when Kit finished, he sat back on his haunches and only then did he smile.

''Twas here,' he said, and it was the clearest Tom had ever heard him speak. 'Here we took her. I shall not forget.' He laid the flowers over the box.

And they were surrounded. All around them loomed the Samdhya, in human form. They could not get past them if they wanted, each one carrying a sword or a spear.

Rohenga strode forwards, all panther litheness. Kit tensed, and appeared to accept that this would be the moment he died. It was too fast for Tom or Zita to try to do anything about it.

But when Rohenga reached Kit, he kneeled too.

'We can forgive,' he said. 'And we forgive you, Christopher Last.'

An expression of relief spread over Kit's face that Tom would remember for ever.

Standing, Rohenga faced Tom. 'Already the world begins to heal. Already the darkness recedes. Now the Wildlord acknowledges you, Thomas Swinton. You are a Swinton still. Remember that. Remember the Wildmark. Remember. You know who you are. But you do not know who you may be.' The sound of war drums began to beat. 'There is a balance, Thomas Swinton. You can keep it, or you can change it. Remember.' The Samdhya hissed as one. 'We will watch, and we will see and know.' There was a whirling of fur and claw and beak. 'You must promise, Thomas Swinton. You must promise not to become what you could become.'

A cloud passed over Tom's mind and he saw himself, ravaged, ancient, powerful, standing in the centre of a whirlwind of gold.

He shook himself out of the vision and grabbed onto Zita for support.

There was nothing but trees and the cut flowers lying limply on the forest floor. The box had gone.

That night they played the gramophone, all the records, one after the other, and broke into the port. They feasted on the pasta and tuna and anchovies and pears and plums. Tom unearthed a bottle of very dusty champagne in the cellar. He popped the cork, and they drank it from chipped china mugs. Kit had never tasted champagne before, and he spluttered out the first mouthful. Then they took it with them as they danced through the rooms, the music surging through the walls, swaying and laughing and joking and teasing and pushing each other and stumbling. Leana, disturbed by the unusual activities, slunk away to the sitting room and curled up on the cushions there.

They talked and danced until the sky lightened. Zita, egged on by Tom, did the Charleston and tried to teach Kit, who blushed so deeply Tom thought he might never stop. Though loosened by the port and the champagne, Kit still didn't speak much; but Tom could see that he felt the same, that the blackness had gone.

At last, near dawn, they fell asleep where they were sitting, in the window seat of Tom's room, feeling that they could never be torn apart, that nothing could ever come in between them.

Later, Tom woke, feeling a lightness in his limbs. He could see Leana out on the lawn, pottering about after squirrels. He stretched, enjoying the warmth of the summer sun on his face, and remembered a time not long ago when he had also stayed up all night.

He couldn't quite believe it. Jack was gone. The photograph of his parents was by his bedside; he picked it up and kissed it.

His bedroom was a mess. The empty bottle of champagne lay on the floor by the door. Three mugs, higgledy-piggledy on the chest of drawers. The curtains were wide open, swirls of dust caught in sunbeams. He washed in the porcelain sink, glugged a glass of tap water, pulled on some clean clothes and then went down.

The heaviness that had enveloped the house had lifted. He practically pranced along the corridor and down the stairs. But nobody was about, and there was a curious stillness in the air. Not even a kettle boiling on the range.

After he'd mucked out, fed and watered the horse, and let him into the field, he came back into the kitchen, checked there was enough in Leana's bowl and made some tea for himself. He took it into the hall to drink it in the sunlight by the window.

Zita was reclining on some cushions on the floor, the gramophone quietly playing jazz. Kit was leaning against the wall, clad in his customary black. *Of course*, thought Tom, *he won't have any other clothes*. The grandfather clock was chiming ten o'clock.

'Breakfast?' said Tom. 'I can't remember when I last had a proper breakfast. Eggs. Sausages!'

Kit glanced mournfully up at Tom.

'What's the matter?'

'There be a hole,' said Kit, 'in Long Pightle fence.' Then the boy was silent once more and started fiddling with his collar.

'We've been talking…' said Zita. She swallowed the end of her sentence. They were both hunched, heads drooping.

Tom felt a wrench in his chest. He clutched the back of a chair. They were going to leave him. He was going to be left alone again.

'I do not ken this mad world. I cannot live out there.' Kit spoke carefully and lankily unfolded himself from his position, indicating the outside world with a nod of his head.

'I'm not sure about it either.' Zita suddenly sounded exactly like a schoolmistress. 'What on earth would I do? And at the same time, you can't stay here, Tommy boy. You've got a year left at school, haven't you? You'll be going back and then to the Varsity and everything.' She tapped her fingers against her lips. 'Who knows, you may even end up a QC.'

What is this? Tom thought. They had planned out his future for him? What did they think, that he would return to his previous life, meekly? When he'd just discovered the world of magic, when he was sensing the edges and contours of the powers that had opened up to him, like a flower after a storm…

Zita mistook his angry look for one of reluctance. 'You *should* end up a QC, darling. Won't your guardian want you to do something like that? Or there's the City, isn't there? Or he'll want you to work with him in Hong Kong, isn't that how things are done? You don't want to stay here, with us, in this place. And we, presumably, can't stay here without you.'

Silence, blowing through the house. The sound of Leana's claws on the flagstones as the lurcher surged into the room

247

and curled up by Zita. Zita's eyelashes, fluttering. Kit's long slender hands, clasped tightly in front of him.

Tom didn't want any of that. All of it came back to him, the endless meetings with tutors and advisers, the terse notes from his guardian, the school reports, the questions about what he should do, what he would do, what his future was. Fletcher putting the cap back on his fountain pen and giving him a hard stare.

'It's not what you want, darling.' She was still, the sunlight reflecting off her luminous eyes. 'What we want isn't always what we get. It's what's expected of you.' Zita folded her arms as if she'd decided for him already.

'You didn't do what was expected of you,' said Tom. 'You left your home, your parents, your future.'

'And look what happened to me,' she replied softly. 'What a paragon am I!'

Zita was right. They would want him back soon, at the end of the holidays. He calculated quickly how long that was. A couple more weeks, at the most, though he wasn't sure exactly how long he'd been in Suffolk. Fletcher would be making up the room allocations for the year. His guardian, Hector Tsang, would be portioning out the fees and his small allowance. They would want to know what he'd been doing at Mundham.

How could he tell them? What could he tell them? They would not believe him. He'd be forced to go back, to revision and to muddy games socks and timetables and the smell of lasagne and cabbage lingering in the school corridors.

'You have to do what's right, Tommy boy.' Zita settled herself among the cushions and closed her eyes. Leana placed her head on Zita's knee and yawned.

What's right. What was right? It had been right to stop Jack, who was bent on power and destruction. But what would Tom do? That threat had been removed, and now he had his own power. Tom paced the room and came to a halt in front of the painting of William Swinton, Jack's father, hanging above the fireplace. There was a softness in his face which reminded Tom of his own father.

A glimmer of an idea came to him. Would it work? He wasn't eighteen yet, but he would be soon enough.

He tested the new thought from all angles. He paced the room more quickly. He jumped over Zita's outstretched legs. The more he thought about it, the more he believed it could happen.

'What is it, Tommy? You look like you've had an epiphany.' Zita had opened her eyes and was following his progress around the room. Kit was expressionless.

'I have! Listen – Jack's gone, and I'm his only relative.'

'What are you saying?' Zita looked puzzled.

'Don't you see?' A joy took hold of Tom and spread through him, making him dance. He grabbed Zita by the hands, lifted her up and whirled her around. 'It's mine! The house is mine, it belongs to me!'

'You're right!' said Zita. 'You're right!' Then, as she steadied herself on the back of a chair, she added, 'It might not be that easy. The solicitors and bankers and people – there's a lot of complicated things Jack set up over the years. Trusts and companies and shell companies and Lord knows what else. I tried to keep track of it but I couldn't always.'

'We'll look into it! There must be a way, there must, there must, if I'm his only living relative ...' It was true, it had to be true. 'And where are you meant to go anyway? You said yourself you can't go out into the world, and you can't stay here in a house that isn't yours. So stay with me – in my house!'

'You'd do that?' Zita laughed, letting go of his hands. 'Tommy, you'd really do that? Silly boy!'

Tom felt his heart leap. He hugged Zita and their hands entwined once more.

There was a cough and a rustling, and a black-clad, spindly presence approached. Kit was still weak and he kept having to stop to hold on to things. He grasped the edge of the mantelpiece.

'Kit? What do you think?'

The boy did not need to speak. His once-silver eyes were bright and blue and alive. He bowed his head to Tom and said, 'Master.'

'None of that,' said Tom. 'None of that, Kit! There'll be no master here.' As if in confirmation, Leana leapt up and he scratched her behind the ears until she dropped back down. Kit raised his head and they clasped hands.

They went outside. Leana tumbled around them, a dark flash of zigzagging life. 'Look!' Tom pointed. Across the home field, a swathe of white and blue flowers had opened their petals to the sun.

A hare, long ears twitching, was facing the house. It bounded towards the woods, and by the time Tom had breathed out, it had gone.

ACKNOWLEDGEMENTS

To all the team at Little Island: Matthew Parkinson-Bennett, Siobhán Parkinson, Kate McNamara, Elizabeth Goldrick.

To Antonia Wilkinson for publicity.

To those who read early chapters, and offered encouragement: Catriona Ward, Katherine Kingsley.

I am especially grateful for my Fellowship with the Royal Literary Fund, without which this book could not have been written.

ABOUT PHILIP WOMACK

Philip Womack is a critically acclaimed children's author. His books for children and teens include *The Double Axe* and *The Arrow of Apollo*. The adult nonfiction *How to Teach Classics to Your Dog* was published in 2020. Philip lives in London with his wife, the architect Tatiana von Preussen, three children and lurcher. He spends a lot of time in Suffolk, looking at moats and mounds.

ABOUT LITTLE ISLAND

Little Island is an independent Irish publisher that looks for the best writing for young readers, in Ireland and internationally. Founded in 2010 by Ireland's inaugural Laureate na nÓg (Children's Laureate), Little Island has published over 100 books, many of which have won awards and been published in translation around the world.

RECENT AWARDS FOR LITTLE ISLAND BOOKS

Book of the Year, KPMG Children's
Books Ireland Awards 2021
Savage Her Reply by Deirdre Sullivan

YA Book of the Year,
An Post Irish Book Awards 2020
Savage Her Reply by Deirdre Sullivan

Judges' Special Prize, KPMG
Children's Books Ireland Awards 2020
The Deepest Breath by Meg Grehan

Shortlisted: The Waterstones Children's
Book Prize 2020 (Shortlisted)
The Deepest Breath by Meg Grehan

IBBY Honours List 2020
Mucking About by John Chambers

Children's Book of the Year
(Junior),
An Post Irish Book Awards 2019
123 Ireland by Aoife Dooley

Literacy Association of Ireland
Children's Book Award 2019
Bank by Emma Quigley

Great Reads Award 2019
Dangerous Games by James Butler

Honour Award for Illustration,
Children's Books Ireland
Awards 2019
*Dr Hibernica Finch's Compelling
Compendium of Irish Animals* by
Aga Grandowicz and Rob Maguire

www.littleisland.ie